THE BRONZE CHRIST

Yoshiro Nagayo

THE

BRONZE CHRIST

translated by Kenzoh Yada and Henry P. Ward

Taplinger Publishing Co., Inc., New York, 1959

Copyright, 1959, by Taplinger Publishing Co., Inc.

Library of Congress Catalog Card No.: 57-11184

Printed in the United States of America

Designed by Charles Kaplan

TRANSLATOR'S NOTE

THE BRONZE CHRIST is a modern novel which deals with a religious persecution so severe that it rivalled the cruelty of the Spanish Inquisition and the Roman persecutions of the Christians. The entire episode is, however, almost unknown to most people of the Western world.

Until 1854, when Perry forced the Open-door Policy, Japan had been almost completely isolated from the West and its ideas. Exposure to Western culture had begun—to some degree—less than a century before, and yet even in that short period of time the impact of Western thought had been tremendous. The two hundred and fifty years of systematic and persistent efforts that had begun in 1600 to eradicate the effects of Western influence—and especially of the influence of Christianity—had been wholly unsuccessful.

The first Westerners ever to reach Japan were Portuguese merchants who sailed up the China coast from their trading outpost at Macao in 1542 to open up valuable new markets both for themselves and for Japan. The political situation in Japan for the past one hundred and fifty years had been marked by great turbulence and constant petty feuding. Although the emperor continued to live at the capitol in Kyoto, there was no central power in Japan because he was

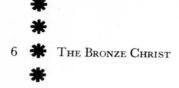

devoid of the necessary power to enforce any consistent policy. In fact, although his prestige was high with the people and therefore a potentially strong political factor, he often had difficulty in garnering enough food to eat from day to day. The local governors, or daimyo, as they were called, vied constantly with each other to become powerful enough to seize the capitol area and thereby be able to utilize the emperor as a figure-head for a central government. None of them was successful, however, until Nobunaga Oda, who took advantage of the new weapons—firearms—which had been brought into the country by the Portuguese. But, just as Nobunaga was about to climax his victories, he was killed by one of his lieutenants in 1582, and Japan was again without a strong leader until Hideyoshi Toyotomi revenged Nobunaga's death by killing the assassin. Hideyoshi was able, with the emperor's support, to control most of the other daimyo until his death, whereupon the Tokugawa dynasty began a long reign which lasted until the mid-nineteenth century and the Meiji Restoration in 1868.

Paralleling the confusion of the political situation at the time of the first Western contact, was the chaos in Japanese society. Morality was at a low ebb and Buddhism, after having flourished for a thousand years, was showing definite signs of decadence.

When Francis Xavier came to Japan in 1549 the country was ripe for the acceptance of a vital religious force and Christianity gained converts at an astonishing pace. Nobunaga had recognized it as a tool which he could effectively use against the reactionary Buddhists and he encouraged the early priests. Even Hideyoshi was favorably inclined toward Christianity until he suddenly reversed his position and published a proclamation in 1587 denouncing Christianity as un-Japanese. However by that time there were as many as 150,000 Christian Japanese, most of them in southwestern Japan. In addition there were many Western priests who had come to Japan in an effort to open new fields for the Jesuits who were losing some of their hold in their European homelands. For political reasons the Tokugawa government tried to check the rapid expansion of this religion by legislation in 1612 outlawing Christianity but their efforts met with little success. Resorting to more drastic measures, Iemitsu, the third Tokugawa Shogun, or general, closed the country to the West by cutting off free commerce, purging the Westerners, and even banishing those Japanese who had ever been abroad. He did, however, allow a certain amount of trade to continue under very strict supervision. Only traders of the Protestant countries, Holland and Denmark, were permitted to operate. In 1637 a two-year war, the Shimabara Revolt, was started. It was largely a war between the Tokugawa government and the Christians and their sympathizers. Iemitsu scored a smashing success and Christianity in Japan was doomed for several hundreds of years.

When priests were once more allowed in Japan during the Meiji Period they were astonished to learn that some remnants of the Christian faith had persisted. A few Japanese travelled to Yokohama from the south to confirm rumors they had heard

that there were Christians once more in Japan. When they found that the priests were indeed of the same religion as their forefathers, they revealed themselves as Christians and to prove themselves they recited their catechisms and prayers which had been handed down by word of mouth from generation to generation for two hundred and fifty years in the face of fantastic persecution and awful penalties.

The Bronze Christ, then, is a story based on that persecution.

AUTHOR'S NOTE

I T I S a fact that during the Kanbun period (1661-1673) there lived in Furukawa-cho in Nagasaki a caster whose name was Hagiwara, and he was mistakenly killed as a believer in Christianity because his treading picture was too well done. It is also true that an apostatic priest Christopher Ferreira, or Chuan Sawano, invented the idea of the treading picture. The various torture techniques and the historical prologue in the first chapter are also facts. Antonio Rubino was a real priest, but I don't know whether those events occurred at the same period or not.

At this point I would like to thank Nagami Nagasaki for giving me an idea which developed into this story. I would also like to record here that I used the following works as references : *Martyrs of Christianity, Revival of the Church of Japan, Nagasaki of the Edo Period* and *Chronological Table of Nagasaki,* all written by Mr. Ono.

I allowed certain anachronisms in this story; for instance, there was no woodblock printer in Nagasaki in the Kanbun period, but, since this novel is merely my creation based on history and not a strict historical novel, I put one in. For those interested in accurate historical data, I suggest a history book.

CHAPTER 1

THIS STORY begins at the time of the death of Iemitsu, the third Tokugawa Shogun, when his son, Ietsuna, took up the reins of the Japanese government. During his lifetime Iemitsu was noted for his cruel excesses toward Christians. Before him Nobunaga and Hideyoshi had each failed to perpetuate their control of the country. Iemitsu, as the third in succession, was well aware of the hopes and expectations of the daimyo that his own family would follow the same pattern of decline; in fact, he himself was not immune from some anxiety over his capability to control the Tokugawa power. However he was an intense young man who had an uncommon intelligence for his age and he hit upon an excellent way of demonstrating in detail that he was capable of punishing conclusively any daimyo who defected ever so slightly from the official national policy—the oppression of Christianity. Many daimyo, who originally thought Iemitsu too young to be an effective ruler, abandoned their own ambitious plans to supplant him when they saw his thorough program of eradication. Even Masamune Date, who was one of the most powerful and ambitious daimyo and Iemitsu's biggest rival, finally changed his lax attitude toward Christians when he went to Edo to visit Iemitsu and saw fifty Christians

beheaded in Suzugamori. Iemitsu took much personal interest and pleasure in this program because, for one thing, it proved so effective in intimidating the daimyo without his having to resort to open warfare and, for another, it involved nothing more complicated than butchering this passive herd who denied Japanese gods and disobeyed Japanese laws. Even when the slaughter appeared to the daimyo to be too cruel they were unable to object because to deny the Japanese gods was a treasonous act.

One day Iemitsu enjoyed special satisfaction when he received an official letter from Masamune announcing that he too was taking strong measures to eradicate Christianity from his area. Iemitsu became so excited by this display of deference to him, it was reported, that he jumped up and childishly dashed in to show his wife the letter.

Iemitsu instituted this program of cruelty not only because of its intimidating effect on the daimyo but also because he sincerely believed that the purpose of the Christians was to invade Japan under the guise of preaching the way to God and redemption. He was neither alone nor unreasonable in this belief. Since the time of Hideyoshi influential Buddhists and Shintoists at court had engaged in all kinds of slanderous plots against the Christians. Besides this, Spanish merchants, who were trying to offset the trade advantage to Portugal, *boasted openly* that Spanish territories had been acquired by using Christianity as the forerunner to conquest. A Dutch merchant, while pointing to Protestant Holland on a world map, had once said to Iemitsu's grandfather, Ieyasu, "Even one king of a Christian country thinks that priests are so dangerous to his country that he is trying to drive them out." The Hollander then broke a crucifix in two and stamped on a picture of the Holy Mother—a so-called "secret document" found aboard a Dutch merchant ship. There were also many philosophical reasons to consider Christianity dangerous. The doctrine that it was more likely that a repentant sinner would be saved than a proud man who had never sinned was understood to condone crime itself. The doctrine that mortification of the flesh was necessary for the salvation of the soul was taken to mean that death was desirable and that therefore the priests who would entice the people to "Glorious Death" would destroy the country itself. Moreover, at the turn of the century there were many epidemics, earthquakes and typhoons. These the Buddhist and Shinto priests were swift to attribute to the anger of their gods.

At first Hideyoshi paid little attention to this sort of talk, but when a Christian girl whom he loved would not give herself to him he began to take a dim view of Christianity. He ordered her stripped and lashed to death with bamboo spears. It was that same General who coined the proverb, "Don't try to grow a foreign tree in Japan just because it thrives elsewhere. We have our cherry tree." This reckless hero, who invaded Korea practically single-handedly, believed that he needed to make just one more demonstration to stop the spread of Christianity, so he crucified twenty-six "invaders" in Nagasaki at Mt. Tateyama. With this began the history of Christian persecution in Japan.

From the beginning, Ieyasu, the first Tokugawa Shogun, hated Christians even more violently than did Hideyoshi. At the battle of Sekigahara in 1600, crucial to the fortunes of both the Tokugawa and Christianity alike, some of the staunchest protectors of the Christians were wiped out. Years later, in 1622, with the torture and execution of fifty-five believers the persecution began in earnest. Subsequently many daimyo who had either been baptized or who were merely sympathetic to Christianity changed their attitudes for fear of arousing government suspicion. Within their domains they began to suppress Christianity. The eradication of Christianity thenceforward became a fixed policy of the Tokugawa dynasty. In the century before the suppression of the Shimabara rebellion in 1638 and the subsequent close of the century, over two thousand had faced martyrdom and thousands of others lesser punishments. With this the Christian disturbance had somewhat subsided.

"Once the influence of Christianity was tremendous—almost throughout Japan," people were saying. "In fact, in 1582, there must have been 300,000 devout believers. The authorities had to resort to horrible cruelties to stamp it out as much as they have. But then they were a stubborn lot. When you look at the way things are now it's almost as though it wasn't God's will that Christianity should have come into this country." Even at a time when these comments were common among the people, there were still many signs posted in the big cities and towns reading :

NOTICE

REWARD FOR

INFORMING ON PRIEST	300 pieces of silver
INFORMING ON LAY BROTHER . .	200 pieces of silver
INFORMING ON REPENTED APOSTATE	200 pieces of silver

**Persons who hide or live with
Christians shall also be punished**

PROSECUTOR

And so the story begins.

*There lived in Nagasaki a caster whose name was Yusa
Hagiwara. . . .*

CHAPTER 2

"Sawa, what did you do with that tiger picture?"

Through his heavy glasses Magoshiro looked high and low in the dirty room in which were scattered many curios. He looked in the closet, in drawers, on the table. One could not help wondering where he had found all that weird stuff.

"You sold it again, didn't you? Without a word to me." His voice was harsh and stinging and his wife felt it as she slid open a battered door, some needlework in her hand.

"What do you mean 'again'?" she asked, "Have I ever sold it before?" Somewhat ashamed she turned to her husband's visitor, Yusa, with a smile on her lips and raised her blue, freshly shaved eyebrows in an expression of confusion.

To her husband she said, "Oh, what's the matter with you? Why do you scatter all those things about so? It looks like a junk shop in here."

"You try to find the picture. I can't." He sat down on the floor on his long thighs, taking away the *zabuton*[1] which seemed to get more uncomfortable the more he used it. With the end of a *kiseru*[2] he drew toward him an iron Korean

---

[1] *zabuton*: an ornate cushion.
[2] *kiseru*: a tobacco pipe.

tobacco box decorated with silver and gestured toward one particular picture. "It is far better than that one. I tried to make a good caricature—the idea came from a tiger at the last temple festival."

The picture which Yusa happened to be looking at was an original woodblock print of Nagamasa Yamada showing the famous admiral riding on an elephant as he prepared for his marriage to a daughter of the King of Siam.

"Here it is! You were the one who lost it!" Somewhat triumphantly Sawa handed the picture to her husband and disappeared into the next room.

"Oh, yes," said Magoshiro, looking at the picture as though he had just recovered a treasure. "Come and look, Yusa. The light is better over here." He handed the painting to Yusa and sipped a cup of tea which had grown cold. Wiping his glasses on his kimono sleeve, he studied Yusa's face closely.

The tiger show had been very popular about ten days ago at the festival of Suma Shrine. Magoshiro's picture showed a cage on the street.

HUGE KOREAN TIGER
W E L C O M E * * W E L C O M E

Adult	. . .	1 mon
Child	. . .	½ mon

With such a sign a man was trying to gather a crowd. In another part of the picture, in front of the caged tiger which glared solemnly at the people, was a red-headed man with blue eyes who was strolling arm in arm with a Japanese prostitute carrying a western-style parasol. On the man's back was written the word "Dutch." A red-bearded Russian with a big nose was watching the crowd instead of the tiger. He had a stick on his arm and he was nonchalantly smoking a pipe. Next to a *samurai*[1] with his twin swords, two children were playing, one Japanese and the other Chinese.

"Yes, it really is quite interesting." The humor of the scene made Yusa smile in spite of himself.

"It's the best I've done recently, I think," said Magoshiro smiling with deep wrinkles on each side of his twisted mouth.

Yusa had to admire the picture even though he hated its vulgarity. "It is amusing. Have you thought of making a woodprint out of it? I was thinking the tiger alone would make an interesting subject for another picture."

"Of course. Do you think I would pass up such good material?" He packed his kiseru with tobacco and continued. "It probably seems odd to see the word WELCOME in front of a tiger sitting in the open street, but it makes for an interesting picture." He smiled again.

Yusa was more surprised by Magoshiro's talent than unappreciative of it—more than he actually admitted to himself. What an odd person, he thought. He was not at all satisfied with Magoshiro as a man, just as he was not satisfied with

---

[1] *samurai* : a member of the military class in feudal Japan; a warrior.

him as a painter. Magoshiro was living only according to his whims. Yusa himself could not do that. A person who lives only by whim is nothing more than a limited eccentric who can never achieve any real depth. "Even when I paint or carve for pure enjoyment, I'm never satisfied until the amateur quality has disappeared and the 'whim' has been replaced by something from my heart—until I produce something that will make a million hearts pound." Yusa couldn't deny that Magoshiro's pictures were very interesting, but art which is merely "interesting" can never be more than second-rate. "But I, who yearn to be the best, have never actually produced one thing that even showed a sign of first-class talent. Furthermore, Magoshiro has already realized his own medium and style, which is admittedly interesting. He has the distinction of being the only woodblock painter in Nagasaki at this time. Everyone can recognize his touch in such pictures as *Nagamasa Yamada* and *The Tiger*. He steadily goes along his own narrow little way without looking to one side or the other, while I, who appreciate a type of art he could never comprehend, have never created anything to indicate my wide understanding and the burning enthusiasm in my heart. At least Magoshiro paints many pictures using his narrow vulgar tastes and he never feels restless." Thus even though Yusa did not respect Magoshiro, who was forty and looked ten years older, he was still jealous of him and recognized an empty quality in his own works; they were not even "interesting."

"I guess I'm just interested in too many things." Yusa said.

He sighed involuntarily and looked out upon the small untidy yard with a banana tree and its broken, forlorn leaves.

"It's all right to be interested in a lot of things. That proves you have a good eye," Magoshiro said.

Yusa wanted to agree with him but lack of proof always kept a doubt alive. Until he had the actual proof in his hands he would never feel satisfied, but always vacuous, for he suspected that his confidence was merely that illusory self-sufficiency which everyone has about himself. Since he could never be sure about himself he didn't dare scoff at others for not realizing their fullest talents.

"Nevertheless, I pray that I will develop along one single path, whatever it may be. I can't help hoping—but what if I can't?" Yusa's knees trembled as he spoke.

"Should you ever sink to doing such lowly work as mine, you would be far from satisfied, wouldn't you? You feel that you can do much more imposing work than this childish stuff —which is only good for one or two mon in the marketplace. My work is only for poor ignorant children—beggar's work. But do you realize that I have to exert myself to achieve even just that? For instance, this foolish picture here was harder to do than it looks, and even though I put much effort into it the result looks like mere child's play. On the other hand, you'd be surprised how many people buy these stupid pictures for one or two mon. Of course, my best customers are grocers and fishmongers. They are my public. But that's fitting. For them I *should* be a beggar painter, and I am needed. Fancy courtesans are not the only ones in the world, you know;

there is also a demand for *yotaka*[1]. Is that what you want to
be—a yotaka?" Magoshiro laughed, showing his dirty black
teeth stained with tar.

Even though Yusa wanted friends badly, he didn't want
Magoshiro for a friend. Such low, vulgar cynicism repelled
Yusa. Magoshiro interpreted the feelings of everyone in his
own superficial, cheap way and ridiculed them as if he knew
everything. Whenever someone justifiably criticized him, he
replied, "Don't shout!", even though they hadn't raised their
voices, and then he would laugh mockingly. When he laughed
it was invariably with a deliberate sneer. "This man who feels
so superior by belittling everything can smile when no normal
person can," thought Yusa. "If you ask him what is so funny,
he merely replies, 'Everything is funny. I myself am funny,'
and he laughs again. Of course, he doesn't really think anything is funny. He just likes to keep laughing and tries to
make himself think things are funny. That's why he drags
everything down to his own low level of understanding. No
wonder people don't like him. The more people are angry at
his manner, the more satisfied he is with his cynicisms, and
then he smiles smugly as though he doesn't know why they
are annoyed. This is his 'victory.' But when you listen beyond
his venomous tongue you can see that his cynicism is not just
on the surface. His self-sneering, which looks as cold as ice
from the outside, is just a thin veneer over annoying barbs.
Deep inside there is the weak, lone fire of a twisted person. At
least the fire gives his blue face a reddish tint."

Aloud, Yusa said, "Nevertheless, you are a painter and I

am not yet one." Despite his hatred of Magoshiro's way of using the word "yotaka," his sympathy showed in his excited face.

"Yes, even though I do very low work, I am a painter. I am a painter-merchant, no more. But you—you must be different because you have good blood. But then you are still young. Don't be in such a hurry." He spoke without any tone of kindness and, as though he were bored, he looked around and said, "What's happening with that *Matabeh*-like[2] picture of yours? Is it coming along?"

"No, no good at all." Yusa replied shortly because he resented Magoshiro's not calling it just a portrait but having to say "Matabeh-like." Magoshiro paid no attention and went on.

"You have no interest in casting? If you could do it like your father, I'm sure you would be the best caster in all Japan."

"Yes, I know, no one else knows the process yet," Yusa said making clear Magoshiro's implication.

"If one had the talent to master it, it might be amusing. Probably some people could do good things with even it." Magoshiro spoke as if to say he would be very successful with it if he knew how to use it and he started to rub his chin.

"I agree with you, but for me. . . ."

"I see. Not enough of a challenge? What ambition!" Magoshiro yawned in expression of his only attitude.

---

[1] *yotaka* : a night hawk; colloq. for streetwalker or prostitute.
[2] *Matabeh* : a Japanese painter (1578-1650) of the Tosa School.

A voice came from outside and a neighbour opened the entrance door. "Come on out, Sawa! Here come the girls again!"

"Oh, my goodness, I didn't realize it was so late," the wife said and opened the door. "Hagiwara-san, don't you want to come and watch it too?" she asked Yusa as she wound a ball of yarn, holding the string in her mouth.

"What are you talking about?" Yusa asked.

Magoshiro replied, "The Maruyama girls, of course," as if to say, "You know very well what she means, why ask at all," and he added out loud, "There is a chance you might like them. There are no Christians among them." He winked at Yusa and stood up.

"But I don't think it would be very good for you. It is a bad influence," said Sawa on her way out, and Yusa quickly lowered his eyes.

While the government was generally very strict with foreigners it was also very soft with them in some ways. For instance, it sent many Maruyama girls to the island of Dejima off Nagasaki (on which it obliged foreigners to stay) to buy the Redheads' good will. Even on rainy days so dark that people would use lights, thirty or forty prostitutes wearing thick white powder that seemed as if it might flake off at a touch would be urged onward and marched off by guards to the island. The next morning they would return with gray, spiritless faces, quite changed from the day before.

"Well, I think I had better go this evening, since I have to paint it," said Magoshiro.

"What are you going to paint?" Yusa stood up, vowing never to visit him again.

"I want to paint the Dutch Quarter—the dissipating Redheads at play." Magoshiro put on an overcoat, took his sketchbook to his chest, and somewhat excitedly arranged his painting materials.

With a lightning-quick glance at her husband Sawa warned Yusa, "Be careful. Don't let him tempt you."

"Hah! Me tempt him? What a laugh!" Magoshiro said and glanced at the youth again. "Would you like to go with me—my little virgin?"

"No thank you, I have to go now. See you later," Yusa said to Magoshiro's wife and disappeared into the evening crowd. . . .

CHAPTER 3

"I AM too weak. Why do I try to make such friends, even when I know it's no good?" He repeated this question to himself again and again. Glancing back many times as he walked, he could not rid himself of the feeling that Magoshiro was peering through the crowd at his back with a sarcastic smile on his pale little face. The imagined gaze made his body squirm as if he had an itch. He imagined Magoshiro saying to his wife, "Did you notice the glint in his eye as he watched the march? How can *I* tempt *him*? Oh, that hypocrite!" Yusa was frightened by the idea of such a destiny but he lacked the willpower to prevent it.

Try as he would, his pace became slower. His walk was something like the movements of a tired person who falls asleep just when he tries his hardest to stay awake, and an indefinable loneliness covered his head like a heavy black cloud. It did not matter that Magoshiro had no faith in him. After all, Magoshiro was not a good enough person to really understand him. But he felt that behind Magoshiro's cold-blooded face was hidden the face of Fate. Yusa tried to convince himself that it was only because he was thinking too much that he could not shake off the uncomfortable phantom which was fixed in his mind. But it was no use. He could not

believe that Magoshiro's face was just *Magoshiro's* face; he could not believe that his sarcasm was just *his* sarcasm. He feared he would be impotent against Fate. He feared the words, "You're helpless!" and a demoniacal laugh would echo back resoundingly with an awful tone. He beat the hard earth with his feet, looked up at the sky, and cried out with no voice, and kept on walking.

The street was filled with men's voices thrown toward the prostitutes' line and the wild voices of women. Not able to bring himself to look at the line, he instinctively turned into a side street. But where to? He did not head toward home. Halfway up Hikoyama hill was the old house built by his father. The morning sun always shone well on that house where Yusa was living with a divorced aunt. Only with the sun shining on the house was it his warm home and studio in which he could relax and feel comfortable. He didn't feel at all lonesome when he lived close to *Gigeiten*,[1] his muse, who had settled in his house. In fact, he even enjoyed his solitude in that house.

But that place was only for daylight! After the sun went down behind Mt. Inasadake many lights began to twinkle in the lower town and when the cold wind blew into his house through the holes in the *shoji*,[2] there was born a new disturbing world for him and his serenity vanished.

Two or three stars shone invitingly in the sky and lights began to shine on the earth tempting him with a fresh feeling,

---

[1] *Gigeiten*: the diety of the arts.
[2] *shoji*: paper sliding doors.

as when a baby opens his eyes in the early morning. With the night, uneasiness and loneliness, thrills and suggestions of darkness came over him like demons and caught his heart. To be caught by a demon is an awful agony, but at times it can also be a cold joy. Something forced his young heart to boil with an irresistible power and even Gigeiten, who was noble during the daytime, now became amorous and coquettish with dancing and lured him out into the night. Even just to think about returning to his house was painful and horrible. He must become completely exhausted in the world of night before the idea could be in the least palatable.

Toward the beach near a huge pier he shivered from a cold autumn wind which came from the seaside, heavy with the smell of salt. He had not even noticed the Chinese curio shop in which he usually stopped. The beach was deserted in the November quiet and over the blackness the cold wind joined the autumn tide as it shook the houseboats like leaves in the water and rose as high as the shoreline road. He reached the seaside and sat down.

In a huge house extending over the sea to his right, one big room, in bold square relief against the dark sky which was flecked with many tiny stars, shone inconceivably bright. Certainly in that room was daylight far brighter than daylight itself. But what an exaggerated and restless brightness! There was none of the peace and happiness of a human being's house. Many clusters of darkness, darker than the night, surrounded the big bright room, like black waves washing the foot of the island. From the room the music and songs

of a joyless celebration blared out together with the dry and dreary voices of laughter. That house on Dejima Island was called the "Dutch Quarter."

Yusa began to walk toward the strange house, looking around furtively from time to time for Magoshiro. Since no one was allowed to go there except foreigners, prostitutes and Buddhist priests, he could not imagine Magoshiro's getting in. One needed a boat to cross the narrow strait and the ferryman was one of the commissioner's samurai. "No doubt he lied. He wouldn't go there just to paint a picture," he thought, but still he looked behind him and was suddenly frightened by what he thought was a huge white face on a long neck. He shook with fear but an uncontrollable fascination for dreadful things made him look back again. It was actually just a sign-board standing behind a small policebox with a message that seemed to have been written by some devil:

INFORMING ON PRIEST	300 pieces of silver
INFORMING ON LAY BROTHER . .	200 pieces of silver
INFORMING ON REPENTED APOSTATE	200 pieces of silver

If they are found in your home or if it is found that you hid them you will be punished.

"Who's there?" A samurai walked up to him, rubbing his arms from the cold. Yusa did not answer. "Who's there?"

"A caster."

"What is a caster?"

"An artist who casts in bronze."

"Casts in bronze? Well, tell me, what do you make?"

"Oh, I can make anything. A Mt. Fuji—even your head."
He felt like being sarcastic.

"You come here from time to time, don't you? Would you like to go over there on the island?"

"Yes, I would like to see a girl, but I won't go there just so you can arrest me." As he turned to leave he could hear the wanton voices from the Dutch Quarter which was so close he could almost touch it. He heard the scream of a girl followed by loud steps and a flowerpot come crashing down from an upper window with a loud noise as it broke on the stones below. After a while the quiet returned and he saw the small face of a Japanese girl cuddling a cat in her arms in one of the windows and next to hers the face of a monstrous man who had matted hair all over his body. The man bent over the girl and with the laughter of two people who have just made up, they drew a red curtain across the window.

CHAPTER 4

"I BET you are one of these. Are you?" The girl drew the sign of the cross on her knee with a pudgy index finger.

"What's that?" The man watched her face in wide-eyed astonishment.

"This!" The girl drew it again. "You know very well what it is, don't you?"

"Christian?"

"Shh!" the girl stopped him, startled at the loudness of his voice. She frowned and turned to see if there was anyone nearby. She gave a sigh of relief and nodded slowly, looking deeply into his eyes.

"Me? Why?"

"Just had a feeling. Am I right?"

"No, as a matter of fact, they think I am a heretic."

"Oh, you are just saying that to avoid talking about anything holy when you are in a whorehouse. It might spoil the whole evening."

"But I really don't believe in holy things as they do."

"Oh? Why?" she asked, still watching his eyes.

"Why? Because I don't like Christianity, that's why," the man said, lowering his voice. "Because they believe that anyone who doesn't belong to their little group is lower than a

human being; they think he has no conscience at all. There is nothing more nauseating than false modesty and hypocrisy."

"Yes, you are right. I have been disappointed in the Christians lately. They are cowardly. They have no sincerity and they think they should be saved just because they pray and repent, even after they have committed a mortal sin which by all rights should send them straight to Hell. Right from the start they expect to be saved and yet they step on pictures of Christ! When they are asked to swear that they are not Christians, they do it quite easily. There is nothing cheaper than expecting to be saved despite such faithlessness and selfishness."

"Still, there are some exceptions, but——" the man looked away. He continued, "Even so, remember that the government has been so cruel and strict with them. There is a limit to human endurance."

"Yes, I guess you are right," the girl said quietly. "No one can live nowadays without becoming sly and clever. It's hard to keep your honesty, sincerity and sympathy without being considered stupid. How foolish those old brave believers were! —Oh, it's getting cold, isn't it?" The girl stood up to close the shoji tight. "Fireworks," she said, putting her hands on the railing. "What lonesome fireworks they are." And turning her head to the right she called out to someone, "Hello there, stupid!" and waved.

"Close the shoji and come back here. It's cold."

"You just don't like to be seen here, you sneakthief." She looked at the man and showed her white teeth.

"I think your customer is a friend of mine," he said in some embarrassment. From outside someone was calling to the girl. When he heard that voice, he began to shiver.

"He doesn't look like a friend of yours. Look and see for yourself." With this she closed the shoji tightly and took the man's hands in hers. "Oh, what cold hands." She frowned playfully and curled her lower lip. They sat quietly for a while without saying a word.

"You are a believer, aren't you?" the man asked.

"Me? A believer? If that isn't typical," she laughed. "You couldn't find anything else to say, so you had to come out with such a stupid thing as that."

"I know, but even though you hide it now, you were a believer at one time, weren't you?"

"Do you think I'm that kind of girl? I'm not the sort who would change her mind after once becoming a Christian. But I know a lot about it. Today is the eighth of December, the day of St. John the Baptist. Soon Christmas will be here and then the New Year." She breathed a sigh just at the thought.

"Yes, you are a believer! I am a prosecutor and I can tell at a glance."

"Stop it! Such a thing is not funny and you will be punished." She stopped him short and her eyes flashed. "Do you think a believer would work in a place like this?"

"Well, how about me? Don't you think they'd know about it if I were a believer?"

"It could be. You are a good man though, you know."

"But what about the men who force you to work here?

They are good men too, aren't they?"

"Even a good man who is capable of saving a soul could also kill a soul if the devil got inside him. He could even be a murderer."

"Well, in any case, I'm neither a good man nor a believer. I'm a heretic. But I curse any religion which does not open its doors to someone who has been forced by circumstances to commit a crime."

"Thank you, I'd like to think that way too, but if a religion lets any old degenerate criminal be saved—even one tip of his hair—I don't respect that religion. I respect a religion that locks its doors to a person like me. Such a religion I praise."

"If that is so, then shouldn't Mary Magdelen have been damned?"

"Please! Stop! That is entirely different!" she almost screamed. "She was chaste from the very beginning. Even when she did wrong, the serenity of her soul was quite different from mine. And she truly regretted what she had done from the very depths of her heart. So she was saved. But as for me, my soul has been rotten from the beginning. I have never wanted to regret what I have done—not even as much as the dirt under my fingernails. She and I are completely and absolutely different. It infuriates me when you make such foolish comparisons. Even in my dreams I don't want to be saved. That's the truth. It is my fondest wish to go to Hell, just as I am. I adore the idea."

"If that's true, I hope I go down there with you. I'd be

glad to be with you—do anything with you, go anywhere with you."

"Then come along, and welcome." The girl spoke in a low tone and smiled coldly, making very thin lines on her blue-white face. "Oh, why are they so slow in bringing the food. What's going on?" She muttered to herself and clapped her hands.

"You don't believe me. You don't think I'm sincere, do you?" His eyes burned deeply into hers.

"No, I don't" the girl replied without lowering her eyes. She returned his stare with coldness.

"But just before, didn't you say I was a good man?" He suddenly felt he had said something stupid.

"Yes, you *are* a good man, I don't doubt that. So good, in fact, that I thought you were a believer." The girl looked very sleepy.

"But you don't think I'm sincere when I talk about us, is that it?"

"No, I don't. At least as far as your love for me goes. You look young, but you are actually older than your age. When you talk this way you are like an old man talking through a young man's mouth. There is something unreal and false in your tone which doesn't ring true."

"False? Me? Do you really think so?" Yusa said this with bitterness. He flushed again and lay on his back with affected carelessness. He stared intently at her face as if trying to read what was written at the bottom of her heart.

"I think so. I think I can already understand your heart."

The girl's voice remained cold. "You have a love who looks like me, don't you?"

"What?" He was completely astonished and this time he blushed from ear to ear.

"Ahah! You see. You blushed! You blushed! What do you have to say now? Come, say something." She reddened, too, in her excitement and slapped her knee. She laughed with a laugh full of thorns. "Well? Tell the truth. Confess. You don't think you can deceive my powerful 'blind' eyes. Tell me all. I promise not to get angry. I'm not in love with you so I'll forgive you for having lied to me."

"Forgive me, but——" Yusa stumbled. "It's not true that I'm faithless to you. I can see why you don't believe me, but you do mean something to me. To me you are not just a prostitute, I swear."

"All right, you don't have to go into such difficult explanations. You are still a dolt to me," the girl laughed. "Many a lovesick boy tries to find a girl who looks like another, but who is still different. He doesn't even realize he is fooling himself when his heart is filled with the illusion of his love. But the new girl doesn't like to be loved at second-hand—so he tries to make her think he is sincere; and moreover he hates to recognize his own insincerity. But that's all right; no one can help it. By the way, was she a Christian?"

"Yes, the daughter of a Christian."

"Oh, how miserable. So you were refused, weren't you? Why were they so narrow-minded when you are such a pretty boy? I wish I could have helped. Don't make such a strange face; I'm not joking. And believe me, I don't want you to be true to me. It's better for you to be devoted to something noble like your love's saintly soul in Heaven—not to the remains of a woman like me who am nothing more than a clay doll. I'm sure I'm right and you know it too. So no wonder there is an empty sound to your kind words, even when you try to hide it."

The girl rose and went over to him. He was silent. She blew a puff of smoke from a kiseru into his face. "Are you angry my sweet?" The man jumped up, grasped her wrist tightly and drew her down to him, kissing her white and heavily-scented breast as if he were going to bite it. His eye caught the gleam of a copper medal which hung on a chain around her neck.

"What is this? A medal?"

She reluctantly took it off and stared at him. Somewhat dejectedly she said, "It's a miraculous medal. An old Western one."

"Such a strange thing for you to have." Entranced, he took it over to the light.

"A foreigner gave it to me. Rather I took it from him," the girl said. "I think it was the night before last at the Dutch Quarter. There are lots of things over there I'd like to have. They are such lustful baboons. All we have to do is say we want something and they are only too glad to exchange it— even for our filthy underwear. I got this ring the same way." She put her hand on the table to show her amber-colored ring.

"Oh, how wonderful, how beautiful the color. It feels just like skin," the man said, still admiring the miraculous medal. He hadn't heard her. He stroked the medal gently.

"Because it has the oil from my skin."

"And the carving is excellent too. Is she the Virgin?"

"No, not the Virgin—Mary Magdalen. Do you know how to write 'virgin' in the Western letters? Maybe not, but I do." She spilled some tea on the table, put her finger in it and wrote the word "V-I-R-G-I-N" on the table. Then, cocking her head as if she weren't sure, she erased the last two letters and did them over again.

"You see. I knew you were one," he said.

"Me? Do you think such a holy thing can live in this dirty skin?" The girl laughed and said, "For a Christian to see me do this would make him mad because it's a sacrilege. But I don't care because I'm not a believer and I wear it only as a trinket." She suddenly snatched the medal from his hand and hid it in her sleeve. She stared at him and then composed herself quickly as a door opened. "Hush," she said. A waiter was bringing in a tray of food and sake.

"Well, here's one for you too," the girl said to the kneeling waiter. "Open your mouth." She slapped the waiter's hand as he started to reach for food. The man playfully opened his mouth, laughing greedily as she pushed a small ball of rice into his mouth and laughed at his stuffed face. Then she picked up another and tossed it into his outstretched hand. "Stupid dog, go away. There'll be another one later if you're good."

"Bow, wow," he barked, "Thank you very much." He laughed vulgarly. When he stood up there was an eerie redness on his shining face. He stared at her with astonishingly wide eyes. He silently parted his lips and left, with his eyes once more in slits.

"He is a dog, I'm sure he is. Everyone says he's a spy. I think he came here for the government to find Christians. So I treat him like a dog and let him lick my feet. He really does lick them, you know."

"But I suspect he doesn't like you. He thinks you are a Christian."

"I know he does, so I'm trying to provoke him all the more. I even showed him the medal when he was rummaging around on the shelf where I keep my things."

"Why tempt the devil? What if you get caught?"

"Oh, well if I'm arrested, all they can do is kill me. That's what I want anyway. I never have cared much about this body of mine. I'm not as cowardly as you." She grinned at him and drank some hot sake. "I know I won't live much longer anyway. Oh, there's that lonesome wail again from the noodle-vendor's flute. Did you hear it?" She sighed deeply. "Nevertheless you are a carver—no, a caster, aren't you?" She started dangling the medal and stared at it in fascination. Suddenly she said, "Would you like to have this? If you wish, I'll give it to you. But in return will you make a cast of me using this as a model? Noble and fine? Nothing would please me more than that—because that would make my face like the Holy Virgin's."

"What do you mean?"

"Don't you see? It means you will try to cast me but actually you will be making a statue of your love who still lives in your heart. And the more it is like your love, the more it will be like the Virgin Mary too. Some parts may be like me, but the rest—— Oh, how wonderful that would be!"

"Yes, I will," the man said, seeing the tears in her eyes. "I'll make it. I'm sure when you see it you'll know who my real love is."

"Yes, when I see it, I'll see how sincere you are, but not about me. Nevertheless, if you do it I'll belong to you alone." Again the girl stared at him with meaning and laughed loudly.

As the sound of the noodle-vendor faded into the streets, the autumn night grew very late. . . .

CHAPTER 5

Y U S A   W A S   walking toward his house down a quiet street. The reflection of the morning sunshine on the stones smarted his eyes. His heart was heavy with anguish as he tried to find an excuse for himself. Over and over again he repeated, "No one in the world is more filthy than I! I am the lowest! Even Magoshiro, whom I despise, is more simple and honest than I." He could not help thinking humbly of all the common men who, it seemed, were more worthy than he. He remembered part of a priest's sermon he had once heard. "He who has beautiful shoes avoids walking in the mud; once they are dirty, he is not afraid of the mud." He thought of the truth of this. "Surely my shoes are completely covered with mud. I can't even repent any more. I can no longer feel any guilt." Despite his depressed feelings he knew that this was not wholly true. Actually he was still drunk from the night before—her mysterious and sweet flirtatious glances that caught his heart and took him to the bottomless world of darkness. More tempting than threatening was her narrow forehead with its parallel lines between her brows. The thin red lips, the glistening black hair, the sweet smell of her skin. After much teasing, this girl had said, "Are you angry, my sweet?" and then blown smoke into his face. And the way she had smiled when

she said it. Those things were carved into his brain and would never be erased. Last night was the second time he had seen her. Her name was Kimika. It had begun with one of the Marches of the Dutch Quarter. He had suddenly started as if he had been struck by lightning. "How much alike they look. As though they were twins!" He thought of the resemblance and he was so elated his heart was pounding in his ears. "I can buy this girl and probably cure the anguish of my love for the other." That was his first thought; the next was, "And at the same time I've finally got a good excuse to fulfill a secret desire of mine." But he became overwhelmed by a crushing feeling in his chest. He shook his head, struck his thigh as strongly as he could, and hung his head once more.

That night he was plagued by his repugnant, yet intriguing, plan and he felt very sorry for himself, but as soon as it became light he was up and standing at the seaside with a pale face. A cold wind was shaking his body, a wind which came from the grayness offshore. He watched every boat with dejected eyes as they came from Dejima Island. One by one, they came with seven or eight prostitutes in each. Kimika was on the fifth boat, a brown scarf about her drawn face. She spat out a tired "Pigs!" at two or three foreigners still in their night shirts who were seeing her off from an upstairs window of the Quarter. She appeared to have a headache and was rubbing her pale, blue temples.

Yusa followed the girl to be sure where she lived and then went home to sleep until noon. That evening, for the first time in his life, he entered a house of prostitution. When he thought about Kimika, her image became mingled with that of the believer's daughter, Monika. The visions became one and he felt that Monika's was going to disappear behind the other one, but rather than disappear, Monika's was going up higher than Kimika's and, rising, was growing faint like the morning star in sunlight. The confusion caused by these phantoms pained him to the limit of his endurance. After more than two years, his yearning for Monika had become a worshipping. When it had become obvious that his yearning was in vain, his passionate desire for possession had gradually changed into the calm of a resigned spiritual adoration. On the one hand, he held her in profound awe as though she were a thing high in Heaven. On the other, he felt she was a very unhappy girl and he wanted to care for her with his tender love. That memory! Because of it he had avoided losing his chastity, but now the pure and beautiful desire for the memory could be fulfilled through Kimika. This inescapable mixture of haunting phantoms pained and clouded his heart incessantly. Nevertheless the thought of this prostitute filled his heart with happiness.

She had said, "There is something unreal and false in your tone." She had also said, "You try to make me think you are sincere because you hate to recognize your own insincerity." He smiled inwardly. "She wasn't trying to tease me; she spoke the truth, but look at me! What can I do? What does this 'insincere man' do about it?" Suddenly he shook his stick as if he had just hit upon a good idea and cried, "There is something I can do. I can redeem her, I shall do it! I'm sure

I can, and I don't mind being jeered at by insignificant jackals. Let them say, 'Oh, that stupid boy, he was made a fool of by a prostitute!' I'll draw even more strength from their jeering. It's a wonderful idea and she doesn't dislike me. I'm sure I'm not being over-confident." He imagined his future happiness and a power suddenly sprang forward inside his body. Wildly he threw open the door of his house. Since he had been in a house of prostitution the night before, he tried not to give himself away to his aunt by a guilty and restless manner. He assumed a casual air.

"Last night a man came here," his aunt said uneasily. "He said he wanted to ask you something." She handed him a large calling card with the name Chuan Sawano on it and watched Yusa's face.

"Chuan Sawano?" Yusa bent his head in thought. "I've heard the name—but what was he like?"

"He wasn't Japanese. He's a foreigner and also—oh, no one could stand to look at such a face twice—he has an awful face. He wore a Japanese kimono like the kind government people wear." His aunt sighed deeply.

"Is that so?" Yusa could not help laughing. "And did he leave any message?"

"He said he would come back again." And in a smaller voice she asked, "Isn't he a priest?"

"Maybe you are right. Lately Christians have become skilled at disguising themselves," Yusa said, nodding his head in agreement. "But it is strange that he should want to see me. Maybe he is a devil."

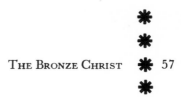

"I think that is exactly it," the aunt said in some agony. "What a terrible thing to happen to our house. How frightening it is. Either he is a priest or a government man. I'm afraid for you. I think he is a devil."

"Look at this. I have something beautiful I want to show you." Yusa took the medal from his chest and showed it to his aunt.

"Oh, you! It is a . . ." Her eyes widened as if she were witnessing some fearful catastrophe as she looked first at the medal and then at his face. She became beet-red and her toothless mouth went "mogu mogu."

Yusa laughed loudly. "Since I'm a caster, any material is important to my work. Look. Isn't it interesting?"

When his aunt learned of his plans to redeem a prostitute, he thought, she wouldn't approve but she would be powerless to stop him, so he couldn't help teasing her a little now. Whistling, he made his way toward the studio, leaving his aunt sunk in an abyss of hopelessness despite her characteristic courage.

He felt sorry for her as he imagined her saying, "Oh, God, he has caught the devil's fancy. He is a Christian and now that means I too shall be arrested and killed." But it was also funny in a way. He pranced about his room kissing the medal a thousand times. . . .

CHAPTER 6

ON THAT day Yusa waited for his visitor until sunset, but when no one came he left his house with a small package containing seven or eight Chinese books containing some pictures his father had laboriously collected. He also had with him a small bronze casting his father had brought from Europe when the government had sent him there to learn the casting process. He sold the books at a second-hand shop in Dozo-cho and showed the shopkeeper the casting which was of the Archangel Michael fighting the dragon as described in the Apocalypse. Indeed it did have a relation to Christianity but it wasn't taken from the life of Christ so most people who were not Christians would not realize its Christian meaning. The statue was perfectly safe to have because everyone would consider it just a foreign art object.

"Oh, it's wonderful! Could you sell *it* to me too?" the cunning shopkeeper said enviously.

"No, it's not for sale," Yusa replied without hesitation. He had originally brought it to sell, but he was sorry as soon as he showed it to the shopkeeper and knew he did not want to sell it. He sighed with relief, took the money for the books and rushed out of the shop with the casting in his arms. "With this money I can meet her at least two or three times!" At this thought his heart pounded with joy.

As he was climbing hurriedly up a hill against the north wind, someone unexpectedly called to him, "Hagiwara-san!"

He looked back and saw a young man running after him. "Oh, Fujita-san!" A little flustered, Yusa smiled with sudden gladness as he turned back to join the youth.

"It's been such a long time! I thought it was you from a distance, but I wasn't sure." Since the young man had been running against the cold wind his cheeks were as red as an apple. He wiped the beads of perspiration from his forehead and struggled to catch his breath.

"Really, I haven't seen you for so long," said Yusa and added hestitantly, "Is all your family well?" He flushed because the lad would probably understand that by "all" he meant one particular person in his family, but at the same time he wanted it to be that way.

"Thank you, we are all fine," the lad replied with hesitation, looking at his feet, and asked, "Where are you going?"

"Nowhere in particular."

"Well, then, let's walk together a while." The handsome boy watched Yusa's face with such deep affection in his large black eyes that one would have thought they were brothers. With a bag in one hand he wore a cotton kimono, no overcoat or socks and a pair of high *geta*[1] on his chapped feet.

"Fine. Where have you just been?"

"I went to town to sell."

"To sell?"

[1] *geta* : wooden clogs.

"Yes," the lad replied hesitatingly, "to sell some artificial flowers."

"Artificial flowers?"

"Yes, because I wanted to have some money." The lad took a white lily from his package and showed it to Yusa. "Since they are not very well made, I can't sell many."

"Did you make them?"

"No, not all of them. My mother and sister and our neighbors make them too."

Yusa looked down and remained silent. Suddenly he asked, "Do you sell flowers every day these days?"

"No, only today, because tonight is Christmas."

"Christmas? Tonight?"

"Well, not exactly tonight, but the night after next," the lad said looking behind them furtively. "But it is very dangerous to celebrate it on that day, so we are doing it tonight to trick them. Would you like to come?"

Yusa was a little surprised and became lost in his own thoughts. "It just happened that Kichizaburo here and I both went to town to sell, and both of us now have some money in our pockets. But my money is to buy a prostitute and his is for the celebration of a holy day. On the other hand, I have good reasons not to be a Christian, and also it is not wicked to buy that girl, for she is the love of my heart and it's just circumstances that force me to pay money. I have nothing to be ashamed of." Thus he excused himself in his heart as so many other serious-minded men do at the beginning of their dissipations. But, try as he would to believe his own logic, when he was walking with this pure youth he had to think of himself as despicable. "Kichizaburo is only three years younger than I, but he still has a naïve face; his integrity is like a straight sapling in the full sunshine. His bright face, his childlike eyes—serene as the crystal stars—his healthy pliant body. These things belong to a man who knows no evil in this world, no sarcasm, who has never known those sleepless nights haunted by carnal passions. He has the serene face of a simple believer. How sickly and wan my own face looks—how decadent beside this lad's." He couldn't help thinking this way when he compared his tired silk kimono with Kichizaburo's cotton one. "This lad is as innocent as a rabbit or a lamb. But what does 'innocent' mean?" Try as he would to belittle Kichizaburo he could find no way of easing his conscience; he felt inferior and uncomfortable. When Kichizaburo asked, "Would you like to come with me." he could scarcely say, "Thank you, but I have to go see a prostitute."

"Me?" Yusa said aloud. "I'm sorry, I'm not a believer."

"It doesn't matter. We will be very glad to have you," the lad said. "But since it is dangerous, and I don't want to cause you any trouble, I won't press you."

"Do you mean to be found out by the government? I don't care about that, but I'm afraid I'll be a bother to your family." Yusa was deeply aware of the thorn in his own words.

"I don't think you will." The lad was somewhat at a loss for words. "Besides we are not going to have the celebrations

in my home, but at a special place at midnight."

"Even so, I suppose your whole family will be there."

"Well, my father has been ill, but my mother and sister are going. If you go my sister will be very happy."

As soon as Yusa heard this he blushed to his roots at being touched on this sore spot, but he wouldn't have had it any other way. He had suffered a deep wound, which had been covered with the resignation of tears and bitter blood, and just recently so, but now the scab had been peeled off again and he bled with much more pain than before. His body jerked in a spasm as though he were going to cry out.

"No, I can't. It would be too painful to both sides," Yusa replied, appearing angry at the lad's kind words, and his face burned like fire.

Kichizaburo closed his mouth and looked hurt, but after a while he said, "I have been completely disappointed in some recent Christians. They don't seem to have the strength to digest the real spirit of Christianity. They just spout doctrine. As a result they are only brittle shells, and have lost all their vital flexibility. If they were just narrow, it would still be beautiful as long as they had strong devotion. Since the end of the Shimabara War the Church has lost its greatness." The youth continued, "But true Christianity must be accepted and loved by people resounding with free and deep convictions or it will die. I faltered once myself, when I tried to give up the doctrine and go against the religion of my family. I had a deep skepticism about this religion, especially about its understanding of the needs of the human body, but now I'm

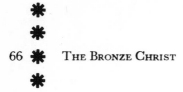

quite at peace with myself and have no conflicts about thinking I am a Christian. A Christian is a person who can believe in the true God in his mind. So I am a Christian."

"Do you really believe in God?"

"Oh, certainly," the lad said with definiteness. "To believe in God is nothing more for me than this—to believe in my own existence."

"You are a congenital believer, but I have no such faith," Yusa said. "And I don't feel the need of it."

"You see, actually you do believe. You are right that it is a congenital thing for man to believe—it is practically his heart—and it doesn't matter whether he realizes it or not. Perhaps you have gathered a few misconceptions about God from certain Christians themselves. This is really strange, because it was Jesus Christ who first made the concept of God fundamentally clear and who correctly understood God as a spiritual existence. For this his gift to human beings is great, but ironically it is through his very followers that many people have got wrong and narrow preconceptions about God. Actually this is quite reasonable, because human beings are apt to personify everything with their own limited understanding immediately, but it is foolish for you to do the same—you who are so well educated. You should not be so mistaken. I don't believe that you can deny the spiritual center of the universe under the existence of which—what shall I say—everything proceeds in order and in balance. Once this center begins to decay, the fortune of the world begins to fall in disorder, not only for humans, but also for animals. The happiness and peacefulness of all creatures depend upon it. When you obey it, you achieve peace. When you disobey it, you are driven to despair. Do you think, when you consider it seriously, that it is just a blind, accidental phenomenon that you are living peacefully and without despair?"

"Yes, I think so. It is due only to fate and to natural phenomena. Many sects and beliefs are created by human beings to make up for their one huge fear—the fear and dread of being controlled by the laws of life and death. Certainly the human being who is born in the morning and dies in the evening, who enjoys only a transitory existence, must have a congenital religious nature against the relentless power of the universe. Without a religion no one can stand against nature. The worship of God or Evil is one emotion which is born out of that religious nature, an emotion which evolves with man's instincts; but even after it has so evolved, the feeling is, after all, just a feeling, a feeling directed toward a phantom and I can't believe in phantoms."

"But what would happen if you destroyed the phantom? Do you think you could still live?" The lad said this with a confident smile. "Without the phantom your life would become meaningless to its very core. Not only would it lose all significance but you could not even keep life itself. No, not for a second! The human machine is not strong enough to be able to exist without it." The lad's eyes were flashing. "No one," he continued, "can exist with complete meaninglessness. Even an extreme nihilist has a nature which can't exist without the principle called 'nihilism.' Even for him, a joy is a

joy. When he does something satisfying, he is happy; when he is empty, he is unhappy. Where does this happiness and unhappiness come from? From his conscience? Then where does that come from? Certainly it could be said it is only a feeling toward a phantom, but for human beings, that phantom is life itself! It is the quintessence of life. For the human body, the sun is God; for the human spirit, God is the sun. For a Satanist, Satan is a perverted god; for a nihilist, nihilism itself is god—and their lives are an approach to their gods."

"In that sense, indeed, I have my god," said Yusa, "but he is quite different from yours. I'm anything but at peace—I'm frequently plagued by despair and uncertainty. Maybe you would say it's 'because I do not live close to God.' On the whole, I think I prefer those unhappy states; I like an eventful life, but it's true that sometimes I wish I were blessed by God. I wish I were at peace—but it is not essential to me."

"It means you unconsciously do believe in God, deep in your heart." The lad picked up a brownish-purple leaf from a cherry tree which had silently fallen down to them. "Nevertheless you are an artist, so the best way for you to have contact with God is through art. Your genius, too, is given by God. I don't think God wishes you to forsake your genius just to become a Christian; as a matter of fact, that would be *against* God, because our spirits are of one spirit created by God. So if you approach your own god it means you are approaching a simultaneously universal and unique god. When you worship your own god, you worship the god of millions. Can one person do more?"

Yusa was quite impressed. He knew that this lad had been a very bright child, but he did not expect to hear such elaborate theory from one who still had the face of a child. He was surprised at his development. The lad continued, "I think it is a pity that some people tend to deny their beliefs, and so deny God Himself just because they do not follow the Christian doctrine to the letter. I am sorry that people are apt to do this though they may be as intelligent and strong as they are conscientious. All people are good if they can feel their own gods in their hearts, but nowadays they think too much about Christianity. It *is* extremely difficult for a person who is intelligent and conscientious to avoid thinking about Christianity these days. The only logical and sure way to be saved through the Gospel was brought to Japan by Francis Xavier. It is the only light and the only gate to salvation in these depraved days. At least the people who have gone to the trouble of weighing Christianity seriously can't think of themselves as unconscientious, even if they don't become Christians or if they don't take to Christianity at all. Some people were baptized because they did not want it to be said —or even to have to admit to themselves—that they were cowardly and afraid of punishment by the government; however, they managed only to show their own empty courage. There were others who had the strength not to be seduced by such a foolish idea of manliness, but became Satanists and degenerated. These are difficult times for a person with a conscience."

"Certainly if there were no art, I would be completely

broken," Yusa interrupted and continued, "But I have completely different values from yours. I'm a heretic in all senses; and not through desperation either. I'm neither a Satanist nor a Deist, but some kind of natural hedonist. I feel no pangs of conscience. I am perfectly cold about religion. It is your job—as a Christian—to decide whether I have a god or not, but for me—I just don't care one way or the other."

"Yes, you are right. Everyone should feel 'I don't care whether it is so or not.' It sounds desperate but it really isn't."

"I don't mean that," Yusa said with a bitter smile, "but I don't deny your good intentions, although you are mistaken. For my part, I wouldn't try to change your beliefs. I'm sorry that you remain a follower of Christ, although I wouldn't advise you to become a completely free thinker, because that is beyond the power of any human being. So please let me stay the way I am."

"Surely every man must live according to his own view of life, and that is as it should be," the lad said sadly. "But you are the only one in Japan who can make an image of Christ as if he were living. Oh, I'm not just being polite; I have unqualified faith in you."

"Thank you very much," Yusa said. "Incidentally, let me buy one of those lilies, if you don't mind."

"Please do. But let's sit down and relax here."

"It's quite pleasant here, but how about over there, near the shrine. There's a pretty tearoom there."

"Shrines and temples are the Gates of Evil for us because sometimes government people come there pretending they are

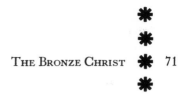

worshippers only to spy on people who are not praying there."

"Oh, what filthy crazy dogs! Well, if that's the case, let's rest here."

The two men sat down on a nearby bench. . . .

CHAPTER 7

IN THE town below, many lights were already shining in the houses.

"Oh, how beautiful! What a multitude of lights, and all put on one by one by human hands." The lad continued seriously, "In the heavens the stars shine; on the earth men put on lights. Many times I come here to enjoy the scenery in the evening and a very mysterious feeling comes over me to see those man-made lights. There is something more in it than merely the act of lighting a lamp because it is dark. It gives me a feeling I want to love it so much I could cry."

"Yes, it's so much like the whole world!" Yusa said.

"Like the whole world—I think so too. I can't stay in it without loving it. I can't stay here without praying. Look at the difference between the cold and too quiet starlight and the lights on the earth. What transitory and lonely lights! They are quite human, disappearing evanescently like foam. How miserable a human being is."

When Kichizaburo said this Yusa felt like laughing and crying at the same time. How often he had come here. How often he had hidden his tears behind his sleeve with deep sighs when he had been despondently in love with this boy's sister.

"I used to come here too."

"Oh, did you? When I come here I feel a solemnity and pathos and I feel like kneeling to pay a tribute. This town has had an extremely bad time. Nowhere else in Japan has there been such spiritual agony. We are still suffering. Perhaps it sounds strange, but I sympathize with this town."

After a short silence, the lad continued. "When I see Mt. Tateyama over there, I feel somehow that I'm looking at Mt. Calvary and I tighten up inside. I think someday I'll be taken to that mountain." He pointed out a black mountain on the right which was half hidden behind Mt. Sawa and which looked like the head of a condor. He scraped the earth with the heel of his geta.

Yusa felt as though he were under the spell of a demon as he stared silently at the black hill and his body almost became convulsed. He had been up on that mountain twice in his life—once with his uncle and once with his mother—both times to see the slaughter of the Christians.

He was only eight years old when he first saw it, lifted up in his uncle's arms over the heads of the crowd. More than ten crucifixes stood there blurred by fire and smoke. A rope on one of the crucifixes had already caught fire; and the tight bonds that were practically buried in muscle were loosened. A child just about his own age had thus fallen free and ran with small steps to his naked mother who was tied to the next cross. She looked toward heaven and bit her lip as he flew to her breast crying out. When Yusa saw this, he could not utter a sound and instead pulled at his uncle's hair. His uncle, who wanted to watch the spectacle to the end, was very annoyed and threw him to the ground with such force that Yusa couldn't breathe for some minutes. Looking down, the uncle said, "Stay down, crybaby!" and laughed scornfully. Still lying on the ground, Yusa pounded on his uncle's legs as hard as he could with his fists and glared up at him with contempt and loathing from the very bottom of his stomach. He cried desperately, "Let's go home!"

"You sissy! That's why I said I wouldn't bring you here." He glared at the boy contemptuously but in a little while he took him back home.

As he grew up, Yusa was educated in the way of the samurai. To be "spiritless and weak-hearted" was the height of disgrace. He also became an ardent loyalist and patriot and began to think it quite just and proper that those traitors be slaughtered since they were possessed with the foreign evil which was trying to invade his sacred country. He enjoyed the game of making and breaking a cross. Another sport he indulged in was to throw stones at people who were called Christians.

One autumn when he was sixteen and his father was abroad he went to see another slaughter with his mother who hated very much to go. This time the torture was extremely cruel, so terrible that they met many people leaving the scene who were faint and giddy on their way down. But this merely stimulated and excited the abnormal part of his curiosity. He said to himself again and again, "This time I will watch it to the end; I will not get faint!" When they approached the

execution grounds, the wind already carried a stench, like the stench of the smoke at a crematory. In one corner of the huge, starkly bare area a great many women dressed in white were hanging by their hair. Their eyes were stretched up in severe pain by the weight of their bodies. Their faces were pale, and from their stretched and expanded hair roots, fresh blood oozed. Some of them bore the additional weight of children hanging from their belts. Around these women, fire and smoke crackled—at a distance so that they would not die quickly, but would be slowly roasted. Opposite them, their husbands, fathers, brothers and the foreign priests were arranged in another line. Someone was sawing on a neck with a bamboo saw, very slowly. In front of one tortured priest sat a big pan of boiling sulfate, and all the poisonous gases were gathered into his mouth by an inverted funnel. His nose was tightly packed so that he could neither cough nor suffocate. He was in tremendous agony. His face was changing from yellow to ashen, and his skin was slowly peeling off.

All of them were unmercifully tortured, for it would serve no purpose to kill them quickly. If a Christian said he would forsake Christianity, he would be released from these unholy tortures at once. The officials tried to be as cruel as the victims' belief was strong, but the Christians in all their severe agony were not allowed to commit the crime of suicide by biting off their own tongues.

"Jesus Maria! Jesus Maria!"

"Deus! Deus!"

"Ave Maria. Amen. Deus!"

The women prayed looking toward heaven with their eyes crazily gaping.

"It is sure that we shall soon be in Paradise; bear with it another glorious minute."

"Don't fear those who can kill our bodies. They can't kill our spirit!"

"Amen."

The believers called encouragingly to each other and under those tortures they returned their earthly lives to God.

Yusa, however, had not seen the sawing with the bamboo saw. When the executioner appeared with a huge instrument, he almost fainted. Just as it began he tried to avoid fainting by watching the sky, the brownish grass, a faraway hill, the trees, the houses. He kept telling himself, "They are traitors! It serves them right." But when he saw the tender flesh of women cruelly butchered he felt a sadistic delight come over him. On the one hand, he was ashamed; on the other, he tried to lose himself in a cruel sensual trance. It wasn't a pleasurable sensation. But when a baby, thrashing violently, was lashed to his mother's belt, he cried out and lost consciousness, not even aware that he had collapsed against another spectator. When he awoke he was in bed at home.

From then on he was known as "the quiet one." He spent his time studying the strength of the human spirit, having seen proof of man's desire to be saved. He meditated on man's worship of God, and how man's thought is terribly strong and unchangeable. He had seen with his own eyes that the human spirit is far stronger than life and death, and that

human beings live not through their flesh alone. Because of the soul which they possess they can afford to receive joyfully agonies which their bodies alone would not be able to endure. From his childhood he had been taught, "When you gather up all of your spirit, nothing is impossible," and he believed it, but he had never imagined that it was as awesome as what he had seen. This new revelation really astounded and overwhelmed him and gave him both courage and sorrow.

He began to suspect that there was something truly great in this religion about which he had theretofore only heard. Even if people are right to call them traitors, he thought, there must be some powerful force in this religion which should not be denied merely because they are considered traitors. He began to wonder, "If their reasoning is as poor as it is supposed to be, where do they derive such spiritual power? Which side is right?" Either way he could not help beginning to respect Christians and to have a good feeling toward them. Also he began to think of himself as a very small, meaningless, empty person.

At the same time some doubts lingered in his mind about this religion. "Why can't they change their religion when they must endure such extreme cruelty? Would they be ostracized by their friends if they changed? Do they have to pay so heavily in physical sacrifice in order to save their souls? Doesn't their God want the universe to be placid and serene? I feel there should somehow be more freedom and more comfort in this human world. Otherwise, God, who gave us these bodies, is too merciless."

He thought further, "It is not necessarily true that Christianity as a religion is cruel, but rather that the persecutors are wrong." Even so, he couldn't help thinking that Christianity must be very cruel and narrow too. "There should be a religion which fits better into this world and allows people more freedom."

He grew up and when he discovered his misunderstandings about Christianity, which formed just at the time he found himself falling in love with the elder sister of Kichizaburo, he felt guilty. Her father had asked, "Do you believe in God and in Christ, His son?"

"No, not yet."

"It is not possible for my daughter to marry a heretic."

And so he lost his love, and turned to art. He scrawled in large characters on the wall of his room : "My Muse Shall Be My Wife!"

CHAPTER 8

''HERE IS another government sign. Do they bother you at all?'' Yusa was too deep in thought to look around to see if anyone was listening to his conversation with this Christian.

"Not any more, because I'm so used to it," the lad replied, but perhaps he understood Yusa's heart. "It is getting late. I'd better go now." He then stood up and carefully looked all about. "The special reason I invited you tonight is that I want you to meet someone."

"You want me to meet someone?"

"Yes, an Elder who escaped from Amakusa after eight years; he's a truly great man."

"I might possibly try to be there, but when and where will it be?"

The lad whispered something in his ear and departed.

Yusa's heart was dark as he watched Kichizaburo's disappearing back. "I'm sure I won't go," he thought. Of course he very much appreciated the lad's kindness and warm sympathy. Obviously, Kichizaburo was very sorry about his disappointment in love and was encouraging him not to give up. Kichizaburo had offered him many comforting words, but the only words he wished to hear were, "My sister loves you, and I'll try my best to help." He felt, however, that he would

never hear those words and a thousand other comforting and encouraging words were therefore not only noisy and disturbing but they irritated his healing wound.

"Oh, that foolish lad! What does some Elder mean to me!" He beat his stick against a stone. He tried to throw the lily away, but he could not, so he crushed it in his hand as he stood up.

"I have to forget all this. The only thing for me is to go there!"

As he was descending the stone steps, he heard a man's voice coming from the same direction in which Kichizaburo had left. The man was saying, "I think all men have 'no' at the ends of their names, like Juwanno, Karano, Migerino; and for the women it is 'na,' like Jiwanna, Kukana, and Elizabena." Yusa stopped short, knowing the voice very well. The man followed him in the dark and said, "Oh, you are Hagiwara, aren't you?"

"Yes, and you?"

"Me? Can't you tell? I'm Tomii Magoshiro."

He took off his hat and the tone of his voice said, "you know very well; don't try to kid me."

"I just came from your house, Yusa. Your aunt claims that you don't spend every night at home." Magoshiro laughed silently, opening his toothless mouth. "Don't worry, my boy. I told her not to worry because you are a very well-behaved young man. Eh? But we do meet in strange places, don't we? Where are you going this time?" He scrutinized Yusa's dress intently and continued, "You are quite a dandy tonight—

quite different tonight than when you come to my house."
He rubbed his chin significantly with his hand as if to say,
This must mean you're going to Maruyama.

"I'm going to Maruyama. Is that what you want to know?"

"Indeed, it is very interesting to find that you, who look
like a true gentleman, are going to such a place as that on the
sly."

Yusa tried to leave without saying another word. It was
obvious that Magoshiro thought him a liar and a hypocrite,
but he had never told Magoshiro nor any other person that
he had never gone to such a place nor ever slept with a
woman. If one lies and says he has never done something
when he has, then he is a hypocrite. To be silent when others
shamelessly and sluttishly talk without restraint is neither
hypocritical nor prudish.

A confession should be made only before one's own God;
it should not be made indiscriminately to just anybody, especially not to a man like Magoshiro. "If there were any
reason to confess, I would be glad to do so. I don't like being
two-faced." He felt very uncomfortable about Magoshiro's
probable comments to his friends : "With that face you would
not expect"—on and on—with no understanding of Yusa's
psychology at all.

Magoshiro suddenly changed his expression and said,
"Nevertheless, I've just dropped by your house. Didn't
Sawano-san visit you last evening?"

"Sawano? Is that his name? Oh, yes, but I didn't see him."

"Is that so? Don't you recognize the name? He was a gate-

keeper to Heaven whose name used to be Christopher Ferreira."

"That's right, and now he's become a gate-keeping dog of Hell."

"Yes, I think your choice of words is quite correct, because it was he who invented the treading picture."

"That device was very effective at the beginning, but nowadays since believers have become more clever, it is not good enough," said Magoshiro's companion.

"However," Magoshiro answered, "it is still occasionally effective. But since the pictures are made of paper, they sometimes get very dirty after hundreds of people have stepped on them. No one can tell whether it is a Jesus or a Mary he's asked to tread on. Even a devout Christian doesn't mind stepping on what he thinks of as just a piece of dirty paper."

"What a really great invention!" Yusa said. "And it was you who wanted to introduce me to that dog? Thank you so much."

"Not really to introduce you to him socially, but now that paper doesn't seem to work so well, he asked me if there wasn't a good way to keep a holy image for a long time by using a casting or a carving."

"Then you immediately thought of me as a caster, didn't you?"

"Yes, I know many carvers, but you are my best friend," he laughed. "Since your speciality is casting and since bronze lasts longer than wood—well, when I told the foreigner this, he was very pleased but said he did not know that there was a caster in Japan. What do you think? Wouldn't you like to

take a try at it? I'm sure you could make a lot of money."

"Sure, so that the rabble can step on my cast? Thank you, no." Yusa turned suddenly into a small street without saying as much as goodbye, but as soon as he was alone he was sorry. "Why did I behave in such a vulgar way?" He thought of Magoshiro's wife who had been very kind to him. He felt he had been stupid and immature to let his brooding and suspicions get the best of him, but on the other hand he still could not forget Magoshiro's sarcasm. "I don't know—he really enjoys doing such things. There is no question that we must no longer be friends," he said to himself as he walked into a house of prostitution. . . .

CHAPTER 9

THE GIRL did not come in right away and Yusa felt very much alone when he went into her room ahead of time, but he brightened more and more as he recognized the many familiar things in the room. Lying on his side he looked at a picture called *Rauma no Gaku*. He could not be sure of the artist but it was from one of the Nanga schools which used delicate colors. Painted there were a gray-haired Chinese and a red-faced prostitute who were amusing themselves with a pillow. It seemed rather modern and showed a light-hearted touch with a trace of vulgarity but it was not a bad picture. "What a carefree person the artist must have been," he thought. But recently vulgarity of this sort had ceased to repulse him and he rather enjoyed the fact that his melancholy heart was becoming lighter. Suddenly the door opened and Kimika came in dressed more colorfully than usual. She spoke sharply and in a low voice.

"The investigation !"

Remembering the many things he had carelessly said to Magoshiro and to his friend, Yusa was frightened but he remained lying there watching Kimika, who stood stock still looking like a mechanical doll. He said, "What ! You're joking, of course."

"If you think so, look at this ! He is looking for you." She

showed him a huge name card of the type only government agents used.

Yusa burst out laughing. "Don't try to scare me by that dog. But how did he smell me out here?"

"Because he is a dog." The girl seemed a little relieved. "Do you know him?"

"Yes, but I've never really met him."

"You certainly have made a wonderful connection. They say he is a former Christian whom they now call Judas. Do you think he came to investigate me?"

"Maybe so. Nevertheless, I'll see him. Please bring him here."

"I'm not worried. I think perhaps it was the other dog who informed this one. It's strange but I feel like teasing him." She stood up and went out.

The door opened again and two men entered. One was a foreigner, so tall he had to bend his head low in order to pass under the door which was about seven feet high. The other one was a short man, a demoted subordinate. The tall man was dressed very formally, but awkwardly. He sat down very slowly and clumsily and then bowed. "I'm sorry to interrupt your pleasure," the subordinate said in a stiff tone. "This is Sawano-san, very proficient in Japanese, but as I was afraid there might be some difficulty, I came here as interpreter."

"I'm sorry that I wasn't at home when you called," Yusa said calmly although he was blushing. He resented anyone's coming to see him in such a place, as if to taunt him, but as soon as he met this foreigner his dislike changed and he warmed to something in his character. The expression on this foreigner's face was so terrible that he instinctively turned his head, as if he were face to face with a leper. The depressed cheeks, the pale forehead, the temples and forehead pulled by shiny reddish-black scars from a serious burn—his face was frightful. Between the eyebrows and on both temples there were deep holes that looked as though they had been made with a red-hot iron. Their meaning was obvious to Yusa. Among the tortures inflicted on Christians there was one which was particularly horrible. It was to hang the accused upside down, causing all the organs in his body to push against his chest and all his blood to flood his head. Then from his mouth, nose and eyes some blood would trickle but that way the victim would die rapidly of congestion—in as little as seven or eight hours. In order to prolong death they cut small holes in his forehead and temples to let out the blood. Yusa knew about this torture and could see that this former priest had once endured it. But there had been more tortures for him. While suspended head down over the fumes of a boiling hot spring at Onsendake, he had shrieked, "I give up Christianity !" Once having said this he lost his way to Heaven, but the rigid investigation and persecution continued until he had made up his mind in utter desperation to sell himself completely to the high commissioner and to become a bloodhound for them. By inventing the treading picture he succeeded in winning the high commissioner's favor but his heart had twisted. "Since I rejected Heaven, I shall become a Satan of Hell !"

Ferreira stroked his ashen beard and haltingly started, "You may have heard from Tomii-san—ah, I'd like to ask you a favor." Ferreira could only allow himself to steal a fleeting glance at people's faces. He could not look at them directly, as though he were afraid of being looked full in the face himself. He was very correct in his form of address. When Yusa saw through his attitude, even though he suspected that this was the man's way of harming others, he felt a quick sympathy for him.

"Yes, I know," Yusa replied. "I heard. Don't you mean the treading image?"

"Quite right. That is the matter at hand. Could you do it for me?" Ferreira smiled for the first time. When Kimika brought in the tea she examined the two men closely as she greeted them and poured the tea with a smile.

The subordinate said, "To tell the truth we are in a rush for this, because, as you know, it will be time to hold the annual picture treading ceremony at the end of January. If it is possible, we would like to have it done by then. So I thought it would be advisable to ask you as soon as possible if you would consent to make it. Of course, we hated to have to disturb you in such a place as this."

"Oh, really?" Kimika interrupted him teasingly. "But how did you find out he was here. He is still a child and I don't think he tells anyone he comes here—not even his best friend."

"We happened to see Tomii-san and we tried to find him in every house around here."

"Tomii? Oh, that bastard!" the girl said and continued to study the foreigner's face. "Mr. Foreigner, you have a wonderful voice. It would be very fine if you could preach a sermon with that beautiful voice. But—you have had a very hard time, haven't you? You were in severe agony. It is written all over your face, even now. Yes, I like a man of the world; I don't like a soft person."

"Hmm, I'm sure it's easy to tell what I am with a face like this. It is frightening, isn't it?" Ferreira smiled a bitter smile, recognizing her sarcasm.

"Yes, perhaps children would cry out, but as for me I can see your face was wonderful. Even now, as you sit there, other men appear poor and shabby by comparison. But," Kimika lowered her head, "in your face something important has been lost, well, what shall I say—maybe the light of life—or maybe of water. They are completely absent. I'm sure there used to be no such terrible lines about your mouth. They came recently, didn't they? I am very skilled in reading a man's character, but there is one whose heart I can't understand. Him!" With her finger she pointed to Yusa.

Yusa turned his eyes away in embarrassment.

"Look, he's silent! Look at his face, his curled lips. It is his only tricky expression, but he can't fool me. I don't trust such a cunning person." She gave him an arch look. "Sawano-san, please, will you visit me occasionally? Wouldn't you like to? Aren't you free now, perhaps? You're just killing time around here now. I feel like crying when I look at your lonesome, impassive face. Perhaps it seems more so because

your body is so big—something like when a poor person's house is big and grave, one feels all the more pity. It doesn't help you to put on haughty airs and walk around with awesome eyes. Behind them you look like a condemned criminal. Why? You should be respected because of the tragedy and suffering in your past. But according to my prophecy——" She continued to look upward at his face, cocking her head to one side, "I don't think you will complete your years. I don't think you will die a natural death."

"You think not?" Ferreira quietly looked into her face with a slight redness on his pale cheeks and a weird light in his turbid eyes.

"Oh, what a beautiful expression," the girl exclaimed unconsciously. "Oh, it's gone now. It was like a flash of lightning in a dark sky—and something like a Satan I've seen in my dreams, but of course yours was far less fearful than that. Please, please come back again. I've been looking for a person whom I can love with all my heart. I don't ask to be loved in return, but I can't love someone for whom I don't feel real compassion. With a person who looks gentle-hearted but who has only gristle in his heart," she cried, pointing to Yusa, "I can't be in love. From the outside he looks like a good man, but he is as cold as ice." With that the girl asked them to excuse her interruption and left.

"Now about this problem——," the subordinate began with a smirk.

Yusa, who had been staring vacantly into the subordinate's face, answered as if just remembering their purpose in being there, "Thank you for thinking of me, but I had better refuse."

"Why?"

"Because I can't feel the motif. It doesn't seem to fit my feeling at all now, and besides I don't like my works to be stepped on by other people's geta."

"You don't, eh? But since it is to be a cast you could make many copies of it. So even if some of them were stepped on you could keep another one at home on a velvet cushion."

"Even if I made a thousand, they would all be my children, and even if I wanted to make your cast I fear I couldn't do it well."

"It doesn't have to be a masterpiece. All we ask is that you just do one good enough to make believers think it is holy. If it looks like something holy no believer could step on, then it is good enough. The high commissioner's office will be sure to pay you much money."

"We are thought," Ferreira said, "to be people who suspect everything and everyone and it is natural to be considered so by believers, but we are not trying to find out whether or not *you* are a Christian, so don't worry about that."

"I'll think about it, but no one can change the fact that I just don't feel like making it."

The government agents went away discouraged and figured there was only one chance in ten that Yusa would undertake the task. . . .

CHAPTER 10

I T W A S almost midnight, the time of the mouse, when Yusa left the house of prostitution. His head was hot and painful, his body exhausted. Even the fresh air which came from a cloudy dark sky and blew on his hair and face did not lighten the heaviness of his tired heart. "Am I destined to die an ordinary death, without creating, being only steeped in life's nightmare?" But lately he had begun to feel that he might be able to forget depressing thoughts such as these. "What does work mean? Does it mean more to die after a lifetime of hard work, sweat and drudgery, or to die with the pleasures of beautiful, elusive phantoms which one pursued again and again? This is the first doubt. Work is supposed to give you some kind of enjoyment ultimately, isn't it? But when you are about to die what difference does it make whether others respect or despise you? Work is just a way of diverting your own mind, isn't it?" From time to time he seriously believed this, but other people's obvious unhappiness and tneir misfortunes hampered his own enjoyment. He was also troubled because he saw no way to fulfil his desire for enjoyment or deep harmony. How could his happiness and that of other people become one? When Yusa realized the seat of his discontent he suddenly remembered Kichizaburo's words, "It is

because you unconsciously believe in God." He could savor his own enjoyment only when he believed Kimika loved him dearly and although he wanted to become immortal through his work he thought it was all hopeless and tried to divert his empty mind. Wasn't this the reason he was such a hedonist? "If that girl, whom I think I love with all my heart, says 'Let's die together,' I will say, 'Let's go,' but if she were to die I would change. I might even watch her death calmly. I think she was quite right when she said I had no sincerity, that I was cunning, that I looked gentle and good but was as cold as ice in my heart."

Yusa became depressed by these thoughts, then he felt sorry for himself and finally he became angry. "Even Kimika may not be the girl I think she is. Though she has been my only hope and enjoyment, her sincerity may, after all, be no more than that of the ordinary prostitute. I who dream of being able to save her may be no more than a foolish inexperienced boy."

He understood her fairly well and was even glad that she had changed her attitude toward Ferreira from loathing to sympathy as soon as she saw him. In her teasing there had been the ring of truth which he could not overlook. Possibly Ferreira resembled her former lover, or perhaps she had explained it when she had said he was like the Satan of her dreams. But perhaps it was no more than a prostitute's way— to speak ill of her current favorite and praise another. Or was it true contempt? She had said after a while, "I'm not fooled even when you try to make me think you are jealous and

therefore care for me, because I know you are *not* jealous!"
And she had said, "Liar, you are not so sensitive as to feel
pain over such a small thing." Then she had added, "Of
course I would like to hurt you, as much as I can. You should
be tortured more and more, but I can't because I'm too nice.
Oh, I would like to cause you grief, truly, because I love you,
because I think about you." He remembered these things and
felt like both laughing and crying. "If she should give me up!
If I can't believe her heart. . . ." Suddenly he remembered
Kichizaburo's bright smile and murmured, "At least he is
happy."

"See, no wonder I felt cold. It's snowing. The weather has
gone crazy to snow in this area before the New Year," said
the man carrying a hoe.

The other one replied, "Oh, I thought it was just a frost,
but I don't think it will last long. There aren't any drifts. It
will stop pretty soon."

"Yes, it is snow," murmured Yusa to himself while he was
trudging up a dark slope. He hadn't noticed it before. He
looked up at the heavy, leaden sky; big pieces of snow fell on
his face and shoulders, giving him a comfortable feeling.

"Did you bring a hammer?" one man asked.

"What for, stupid?" the other replied.

"Well, let's get started anyway. If we get there and no one
is there, then let's come right back. We can say we dug and
tried to find out but dug up nothing but a dead dog."

"They certainly play some dirty tricks—putting up a cruci-

fix and letting us dig up a cat. But the government started it by digging up the dead bodies for a stupid investigation."

"No, they don't investigate dead ones. They're trying to find out who their families are. But the others are just as queer. I don't think they have to take the *zutabukuro*[1] off a body after it has been put in a coffin and buried. I don't think anyone will be 'saved' just by removing the zutabukuro from the dead."

"They are both stubborn. That's the kind of thing that makes us work at midnight in this snowy weather; but since I'm here I won't go back without getting something."

They passed in front of Yusa with zigzagging steps. Yusa did not feel like going back home. He wanted nothing but sleep—a sleep that would make him fresh and spirited with the glory of morning, a sleep that would toss aside everything into the bowels of forgetfulness. Had he thought there would be any possibility of getting some sleep at home, he would have run all the way, but he knew he would find nothing there except an eternal wakefulness. Just then the conversation of the two laborers aroused his curiosity and he followed quietly, listening as though he were expecting something.

"Are you crazy? The cemetery is the other way."

"Stupid! Can't you see the cemetery over there? What a half-wit you are!"

"Oh, that's right. We took a shortcut—— Hey! There's a man! See that white thing moving?"

[1] *zutabukuro* : a bag placed on the dead body for offerings.

"Wake up. Are you drunk? That's a tree with snow on it shaking in the wind."

"No, I don't think so. Maybe it's a lantern. Ah, there's a new Christian. Great! That's for me."

"What? Are you going to dig it up?"

"It won't be hard. It'll be easy to open the coffin. They don't use many nails before taking the zutabukuro off. Besides there's only a little earth on top of this one."

"But that's only for his family's convenience. I bet this time they nailed it tight all the way around. Look, an owl is laughing at you. Whoo, whoo! He's laughing at you."

"I don't care how tight it's nailed. If I break it I'll get a silver cross or maybe a medal. I'll get the reward money and also some more for selling the silver."

Yusa saw two silhouettes far behind him. They seemed to be two girls following him. They stopped for a minute and tried to see whether the two laborers were going into the new grave. One of them whispered something in the other's ear, pointing to the left. and then they both disappeared rapidly in that direction.

"Maybe they are going to the Christmas celebration," Yusa thought. "But why are they in such a hurry? It is not that late yet." He saw two more silhouettes following close behind but could not make them out clearly, although he noticed one was very tall and that they were both wearing black hoods over their heads. They seemed to be looking in his direction without saying anything but soon they, too, turned to the left.

"What's going on?" Yusa began to feel a deep uneasiness. "Maybe the tall one is Ferreira; if it is, they suspect about the Christmas celebration today." His body shook with fear but he began to walk in the same direction. "I won't go there," he said to himself. "It would be too awful to see her and besides I would only sully the holy celebration if I went there with this filthy body. I'll just look in at the window—only one glance—and I'll guard them from those dogs."

When he turned to the left he saw a light at the top of the hill and thought it was a hearth fire. "Oh, good, and if I go to that tearoom I'll learn something." When he entered the tearoom, where they also served some food, two men were sitting with their backs to him warming themselves beside the fire.

"Would you like an egg sake? It will warm you." The woman shopkeeper who was about fifty with black-stained teeth talked to one of the men after she smiled toward Yusa.

"No, we are not allowed to have any meat or eggs to-day," one of the men replied after glancing suspiciously at Yusa. "Just a real hot sake and a pickle, that's all."

Yusa thought, "Those dogs! What a poor disguise. They don't even know the difference between a drinking feast and a solemn ceremony." He forced a bitter smile and went over to the two and said, "Pardon me, may I have a light?"

The huge man was warming his long thin hands over the fire. His hat was pulled down and his muffler was wound high to hide his nose. He raised his head slowly but suddenly ex-

claimed, "Hagiwara-san! We meet in strange places, don't we?" He greeted him amiably with shining eyes.

"I thought it was you," Yusa replied, somewhat surprised. "Are you working here at this time of night?"

"Oh, mine is hard work. I have some business here," Ferreira explained turning his face to his companion with a twisted smile. "And you? Did you have business in a cemetery at this hour?"

"When I see a busybody I am curious, too." Yusa said after a moment's pause. "I was shocked to learn that there are people in this world who have nothing better to do than to investigate dead bodies." He told them what had happened, that he had come upon the two strange laborers and had followed them to find out what they were going to do. "And besides, I like to walk in the snow. It's so rare to have snow around here," he added.

"Yes, a snowy night is very beautiful, but I'll wager you'll see a more beautiful sight to-night—and it may help the work I spoke to you about a while back."

"What do you mean?"

"Christmas. The celebration of the birth of Jesus held by believers. It is really quite beautiful."

"Aren't you going to arrest them?"

"Well, no. They are not stupid enough to be arrested so easily. They expect us," the other man said. "Also this is really not the right day, as you know, but they are going to do it secretly today. We're not quite sure where however."

"I see. Then you were hoping to find a clue here by trying to act like Christians. By the way, two girls were walking right ahead of you, weren't they?"

"Yes, on their way to Mogi."

The other added, "They often do that. They knew we were following so they tried to confuse us by turning to Chura."

"But I can guess roughly," Ferreira said. "They won't hold it in a crowded place where they might be easily detected. Usually they use a storeroom at the soy sauce brewery on the other side of Mogi for such secret meetings. Why don't you go there; it's time for them to start. I won't arrest them, because we aren't prepared for it. So, we are just going to take a look since there are such large numbers of them."

The other said, "At the entrance to Mogi there is a small path through a paddy on your right. If you find it, there will be many footprints where there should be none. This unexpected snow is a help to us." He and Ferreira smiled knowingly at each other.

"It's a pretty long way to Mogi, and it's starting to get windy," Yusa murmured as he looked through the window. He walked to the shopkeeper, gave her a silver coin as if he were paying for a cup of tea and asked her in a low voice whether she knew anything about a meeting of Christians around there. Her eyes widened as she looked dumbly first at the coin and then at his face.

Yusa went out. . . .

CHAPTER 11

THE SNOW had already stopped. Beyond the point of the pine tree from whose branches snow drifted down, two stars were shining coldly in the sky like diamonds in a deep abyss. Yusa was actually running in his haste. He turned his head back again and again. It was stranger that they were not following him than if they had been. They were too smug, almost as if they knew everything. "They said that the meeting place is in Mogi, but do they really know? If so, why did they need to try to find out from the shopkeeper by pretending to be Christians?" When he considered this he felt sure that they did not know exactly. "But why should they tell their secrets so easily. They don't know me that well." He felt they must have laughed at him after he left. "Nevertheless I must warn them." Suddenly, as he turned toward a house a figure came from behind a storeroom.

"I've been waiting for you, Hagiwara-san," said a boyish voice. "I thought you would come this way. Don't take this path; we'll leave footprints."

"But you must hurry! They are already in the tearoom."

"Already?" Kichizaburo seemed surprised. "But it is all right. I'm sure they don't know the place. Over here." He jumped over a ditch about three feet wide. They then climbed

a six-foot cliff covered with bamboo grass. Kichizaburo gave Yusa his hand to pull him up. As Yusa climbed up from the brush, a bush warbler flew up. At the top of the cliff there was a mulberry field.

"I'm sorry I had to lead you such a difficult way." The lad laughed, breathing excitedly. "Thank you for coming. I'm sure this is the best and biggest Christmas we've ever had."

"Did the Elder come?"

"Yes. Actually he has been hidden in my home for a week. I very much want you to meet him."

"I wonder how he made it here from Amakusa."

"A boatman who is a firm believer brought him and of course kept it a strict secret. He is almost seventy and he has been living on a practically deserted Amakusa Island for eight years. He lived as a beggar while secretly trying to convert a few of the Islanders. I was surprised by his unfaltering zeal and his shining face despite his many tribulations."

After fighting the wind and darkness for some way they came to a good road at the top of a pass where they saw Chichiiwa-nada in all its blackness extending under their feet like a bottomless darkness. On the left they could see the Onsendake at Shimabara, stretching far out to sea like a huge living animal. The sound of the wind blowing was like the roaring of a monster still ravenous even after devouring many people. Far away in the distance, higher than sea level but not like the glow of a star, there was the glimmer of a fishing fire on Amakusa.

"Look, see the many footprints around here. Can you see those trees bent like used brooms?" Kichizaburo asked clutching his collar tight. "The house is right under those trees. You can't see it, can you? If it were daytime you could see only the roof."

"But should it be discovered—even though the possibility is only one in ten thousand—is there an emergency escape?"

"Of course, but since I keep watch on the outside, the possibility of being surprised suddenly just doesn't exist."

The house was quite well camouflaged. It melted into the darkness, and even at close range you wouldn't be able to find it if you didn't know exactly where it was.

"Let's go in the back way. When you enter you will be surprised how much light there is inside this dark exterior, but before you enter you can put your ear to the wall and imagine what is going on inside." Through the thick wall Yusa was able to hear a chorus as beautiful as the ones he sometimes heard in his dreams :

> *"Salve Regina, mater misericordiae*
> *Vita, dulcedo, et spes nostra salve*
> *Ad te clamamus, eules filii Hevae*
> *Ad te suspiramus, gementes et flentes*
> *In hac lacrimarum vale."*

"Can you hear it? It is the Salve Regina in which we ask St. Mary's compassion. This evening we will be singing all

night long, so we sing such songs in addition to the Christmas songs."

> *"Eja, ergo advocata nostra*
> *Illos tuos misericordes oculos ad nos converte*
> *Et Jesum benedictum fructum ventris tui*
> *Nobis post hoc exsilium ostende.*
> *O, clemens, O, pia, O, dulcis Virgo Maria."*

"This is the entrance, even though it looks like a stable." Kichizaburo opened a back door of the cottage which did indeed look like a farmer's storeroom. "Behold! Is this the first time for you? It is also our annual performance." The fire burning in the fireplace bathed the immaculate room in warm light. In one corner a black and white cow, chewing lazily, lay on new straw. In front of the cow there was a tray full of cooked rice and beside the tray there was a manger holding the water of a baby's first bath which caught and reflected the redness of the fire. Indeed the significance of the fire was to keep "the Child" warm. Kichizaburo knocked on a door as if he were giving a signal. The door opened and a veritable waterfall of light surrounded them.

"Kichi? Are you alone?" said a girl in a clear voice. She was standing in the door with one hand on the door handle and looking out of the cottage. She bent her head. There was a small gold crucifix around her neck.

"No, fortunately I am with someone," said Kichizaburo in

good spirits and he looked at Yusa who was still standing there vacantly blinking his eyes in the darkness.

"Oh, is that so?" the girl stepped back and looked down. "I have been worrying about you."

"I thought so. Well, Hagiwara-san, please step in."

"Is it all right?" Yusa mumbled as if he were not sure. "I did not expect to come in. Is it all right?"

"Indeed it is," said Kichizaburo entering. With a look he signaled his sister to urge her to welcome this visitor.

"I'm very glad you are here," she said to Yusa. "Did you have a hard time getting here? It's such a mountainous area."

Monika seemed to be struggling with her words. Her tone was not that of a hesitant young girl nor was it a lisping affectation. It wasn't the calm, motherly voice which can only be heard from the lips of a well-educated, well-bred and worldly wife. Such a voice is neither inhospitable nor vainly flattering, not cold, nor exactly soft. Yusa could be sure only that there was no feeling of hostility in her voice.

"I haven't seen you for a long time," she said, more to her brother. Showing her *takashimada*[1] as she bowed her head, she looked at Yusa whose face had an almost imperceptible blush. She half smiled and turned back again to Kichizaburo. The slight redness of her face at that moment wasn't noticed even by her brother who was no more than four feet away. It was obvious from her takashimada that she had not yet

---

[1] *takashimada*: a style of hairdo with a topknot worn by unmarried women.

married, but the question of why such a beautiful girl had waited so long might occur to anyone. Only her brother knew why she had turned down proposals from believers, not only once but twice. Once Kichizaburo told Yusa that she had a supernatural premonition that she would never become a mother nor die in her bed.

As she was about to rise from her bow Kichi whispered something and she said, "Is that so?" She turned to Yusa and said, "Thank you very much for buying that poor flower. Because you did we were able to decorate at least this much."

Inside the huge main room of the house which had looked deserted from the outside there stood a large pine tree and a tall bamboo. On all branches thousands of red and white candles burned; there were some artificial lilies and five colored papers with the words: *Amen, Jesus, Peter, James* and *John*. High up at one end of the room there hung a holy picture between two candlestands, beside which a priestly old man dressed in black talked earnestly with another man. In front of them many people dressed in ceremonial black with white collars were listening to his sermon.

"Wouldn't you like to join them? The Elder's talk has just now started," said Monika with a light bow on her way out.

"Please feel at home. Don't try too hard. I have to go out now and be the lookout," Kichi said.

"No, it is my turn this time!" A farmer stood up and stopped Kichi. "I can't let you go again."

"But you are old. And it's very windy outside."

"I don't mind the wind and I'm far younger than I look."

The old man chuckled as he put on his geta. By the time Kichi spoke to him again he had already left.

". . . Yes, I've been waiting for this important question." The Elder's voice rang. "But we can live in the world of God with our souls at the same time that we belong to the world of Caesar with our bodies. We can't escape from the governing of Caesar in this world. The way to victory—in other words, the way to salvation—is to accept this fact but to give in to it only as long as our souls are not being distorted or killed. If possible, render unto Caesar that which is Caesar's. When you can tolerate, tolerate and forgive. However, look for the world of God with your soul and seek the right way. We shall be saved then, since the only really free thing we possess is our soul. Even when our bodies are imprisoned—even when we are persecuted—if we can live with our souls, we can be perfectly free and enjoy the feeling of the love of God."

"But they are too cruel!", said a man standing up. "It is not just talk, it is evil."

"Surely the power of evil is quite tremendous now. The stronger our desire to search for righteousness, the more we are tortured, but evil will never triumph. We are being tried by something beyond evil." The Elder's voice became louder and firmer. "We have to make Christ's crucifixion count. If our duty is to be crucified, why was Christ crucified? It decreases the meaning of His act if we have to do it all over again. Martyrs should be respected, yes. But not only martyrs. You must know there are lots of saints who have lived as well and as truthfully under the government of Caesar. Our an-

cestors have amply shown the strength of truthful men. 'Be clever like a snake' does not mean deceit. To love your body deeply is to protect your soul. The soul and the body are not only your own but they are God's and your neighbor's too. Christ did not die on the crucifix without teaching this; love God with all your heart, look for His righteousness, and love your neighbor. At the same time do not do such a foolish and insulting thing as to give your body to an unholy power, but love and respect your body and enjoy yourselves while living under the grace of God. This is something non-Christians do not know. But I tell you," the Elder continued, "the history of Christians which our ancestors made and which we are now making is not only a conspicuous, shining chapter in Japanese history, but it will become a pattern for all people in the world who are looking for a world of God and who are seeking His righteousness. Japan has never shown so strongly as we Christians have that she is as good as any other country in the strength and beauty of her sincerity. This fact will become a deep strength and hope for the Japanese people. With the guidance and light of the great star, Christ, I came as one heart from a distant country looking for this heart—to touch this heart. Like a small star shining on another, I traveled a long way on a dark sea with its rough waves and strong winds and finally arrived here. There was a sunken rock which would not let me land and we called to each other from beach to rock. We screamed toward each other for eight years, but at last your faith crystallized into a single power and brought me to the land and led me here. I'm

now imbued with an ecstasy so strong that I would not mind even death, now that I am cradled in your pure and gentle love, which is like a white lily in your burning devotion. My expectations weren't disappointed. Where else would there be such deep, God-given joy in this world? Oh, there is nothing more beautiful than a true heart and nothing stronger than its power. But, if it does not stand on a rock of truth and if it does not shine with all its might, it will not be strong enough to lead this world. We have to unite more and more strongly under the truth as shown by Christ in the name of God to put light in this dark world and to protect it. Ah, let us love God more and more—God, who let us have the power of this union! Amen."

As soon as the Elder finished his sermon all the men and women crossed themselves and knelt before him to kiss his robe. "Amen, Jesus; Amen, Jesus." At that moment the second door just behind the Elder suddenly squeaked open about an inch. The wind came in from the slit and blew out the lights on both sides of the holy picture. The faces which had been lost in joy and transformed in ecstasy became pale and petrified. No one dared breathe and everyone fixed his gaze on that spot. There two eyes were shining by the reflection of the candles. The Christians stood up, stiff as poles.

"Be quiet," said the Elder as he calmed them. "Don't be alarmed. Let me handle it."

Slowly he turned around. . . .

CHAPTER 12

KICHIZABURO WAS already at the Elder's side to protect him, acting as a shield against those eyes, but Yusa squeezed in front of him.

"Quiet! All of you!" Yusa snapped in a low voice, "and none of you will be arrested. Hurry up. That door over there!"

"Oh, so you decided to come after all," a voice said out of the darkness.

"Come, we can talk better outside. Outside!" Yusa said, going out himself. "A dog has no right to enter a man's room." And he tried to slide the door shut, but something held it open. The two eyes watched the Elder motionlessly—they were the eyes of a snake.

"Antonio Rubino! Antonio Rubino!" A deep tremulous voice came from the darkness.

When the Elder heard that voice, he was surprised and his own voice came in an equally heavy rolling echo, "I know you, Christopher Ferreira."

When the crowd heard the name Ferreira, it boiled with a muted tenseness. "Judas! Judas!" some shrieked and two samurai stood up revealing their concealed swords. There was a whistle and a man holding manacles in readiness stepped out of the darkness to the threshold. Yusa seized his wrists.

"Who are you?" the man blurted out, trying to free his hands. "Are you a member?"

"Yes, I am the leader of this group. If you want to arrest someone, arrest me!"

"Oh, Elder, please, please escape. Run!" implored Monika.

"I'm all right. If a god of the sea wants me, throw me in and the sea will become quiet," the Elder said gravely and calmly but Monika could not listen.

"No, they did not expect to find you here. How can we escape and leave you behind?"

"Listen to me." His face reddened as if he were angry and he spoke in a commanding tone. "I've been hiding myself for too long a time. I have been waiting too long. But what for? Wasn't it to protect you who must live? Hurry!" He pointed toward the door and turning around he walked slowly toward the man. "All right. Take me, my former friend. May God forgive you your great sin." The Elder spoke gravely and spread his big arms wide as if he were trying to shield his flock. Then he returned Ferreira's gaze and closed his lids.

Ferreira became as pale as water and raised his rope quietly without saying a word, but as he stood on the threshold, he fell prostrate at the other man's feet.

CHAPTER 13

About a half hour later Yusa was walking in the pass, away from the road. He was not even conscious that wild roses and sharp bamboo grass were slashing his legs and arms. Like a sleepwalker he came upon a grassy field and lay down oblivious of the wet snow. What a terrible night it had been. His head was ringing with many images—the cemetery, the unexpected strange meeting with Ferreira in the tearoom, the lad's face, the sight of the celebration, which was as colorful and bright as a flower garden in broad daylight, its songs, Monika's face, the face of the Elder, the snake-like eyes of the inquisitor breaking their ecstasy, Monika as she threw herself down before the Elder, the Elder's grave reply and, lastly, the utter collapse of Ferreira. These sights were still spinning around and around in his head. The impressions collided with each other and bounced away again. He could not believe they were anything but a nightmare. "Yes, I am the leader of this group. If you want to arrest someone, arrest me !" He had said that ! Why? He shook at the very thought of it. "I do have some moral courage, at least. Some sincerity and worth." Such a childlike awareness brought a glow to his face. When he thought about the failure of the raid crowned by the crumbling of Ferreira himself, though it was probably

only temporary, he was in such an ecstasy of triumphant awareness that he could not remember clearly what had happened after that. Those people who gambled their lives in a tragic fate, and their tensed faces—when he remembered these, a kind of loving feeling, which is born from within only when one is in such a state of ecstasy, welled up in his chest with a painful twisting and gnawing. And when he began to see a hint of the tragedy of all mankind in the faces of those ill-fated people, his eyes filled with hot tears. As he looked up with wet eyes at the stars in the sky, listening to a storm which had already gone away and which sounded merely like a distant roll of thunder, he gasped as if he had just seen something astounding. And no wonder! His wandering gaze had met a huge crucifix of stars which looked as though they had been artificially placed. He propped himself up on his elbow in amazement. When he pictured Christ on the crucifix, a revelation suddenly flashed in his head like lightning. In front of his eyes there took shape a combined image of the Elder and Monika, more beautiful, more lofty, more mysterious, more solemn than reality. When he saw the dual body shining on the huge crucifix, he fell in adoration, but in the next second he jumped up crying, "This is it! This is it!" He waved his fist in the air and screamed, "Now at last I'll make a holy statue. Oh, I can do it now! Oh, how wonderful! I can make it!"

CHAPTER 14

THE NEXT day when he was awakened by his aunt, it was already afternoon and the bright sun was shining over the city of Nagasaki. Under the perfectly clear blue winter sky, from the wet roofs covered with snow a slight mist was rising peacefully. His aunt was telling him that a government agent was at the door.

"An agent?" Yusa was startled and got out of bed automatically. "Did he come to arrest me?" Suddenly he remembered his impulsive words last night but he rapidly recovered and after thinking for a second he approached the visitor at the door with courage.

"What do you want?" But it wasn't Ferreira.

"Well, nothing new really—— I'm sorry about last night." The agent bowed, referring to his visit at the house of prostitution with Ferreira. "My business is about the matter we discussed last night—because we would like to know your decision as soon as possible. Have you changed your mind yet?"

"Yes," Yusa said. He was very relieved and happy. "I'll do it." And he added, "I was going to come and tell you today."

"Oh, you mean you can? Oh, that's wonderful." The man's smile showed his relief. "Please do your best in making it. The

better it is, the more they will pay for it, you know. Heh heh."

Yusa was tempted to say, "You mean the better it is the less they will pay, don't you?" but he was so absorbed by the prospect of the work that he just muttered, "Of course."

The government agent left after asking if he could come from time to time to see how the statue was coming along.

"How do you like that? Even though he is a devil, be sure to welcome that sort of devil any time. Now, don't you feel as happy as if Satan himself had come?" He asked his aunt playfully.

"Nothing could make me happier. At last you are having your share of luck."

"Certainly." Even as he said it he felt something itching in his chest. He thought, "With this money I can redeem her, if it is at all possible." But his face began to cloud when his aunt said with an earnest look, "But even though you will make money, I'm sorry that your hard work will be stepped on so much."

Such hollow words, Yusa thought bitterly. If she wants to sympathize with me she should think about those Christians who will be obliged to step on it or be killed. His chest was hit by a far bigger and more awful fear—"If I make it, she and her brother will be asked to step on it. Can they do that? I certainly hope so. Even if it is my masterpiece I would prefer that it be stepped on by their pure feet. But can she, an ardent believer, do that?" He felt faint and went to his room to lie down and think. "Because of my work, because it is well done, they may feel more guilty about stepping on it. If they don't it means I will kill her. I'm going to kill my love by my own hand!" The shining hope and joy which had filled him just a few minutes ago suddenly changed to bottomless despair and anguish. "Aaaah—aah." He was completely depressed, his heart filled with darkness, and he sobbed impotently. "But," he again began to think, "she must have passed the picture-treading test many times. Certainly she couldn't have claimed to be sick each time. I'm sure she has stepped on the pictures and repented afterward. Even when they were just dirty, wrinkled pieces of paper, she knew what they were and she endured it." It seemed strange to him to be thinking that way, but it was a very happy and welcome strangeness. "Whether it is a dirty and unintelligible paper or an obvious cast, it doesn't matter; they are holy objects. If she has done it before, she will do it again this time." Also he thought what a clever brother she had and he thought about the Elder's speech. "No, she won't do such a foolish and insulting thing as to give her body to an unholy power. And I will tell them before they go up for the test to step on that mere piece of metal for my sake."

Again his hope was restored. . . .

CHAPTER 15

BY THAT same evening his work had already commenced.

"Who cares whether I am making it for a treading picture or not? I'll make it. I have to—just for the sheer joy in the process of creating." Now his heart was at peace and as he became lost in his work he thought of neither her nor Kimika. Like a man lost in a dark, lonesome field in the evening, who suddenly discovers the light of a house, he sat at his desk intent on nothing except his goal before him, and drew many rough sketches. Without going out at all and without even sleeping for three days, he completed his preliminary sketch. Immediately he started to make a clay mold and next he began the melting of the bronze. He was amazed at himself and wondered where all his energy came from.

As his work progressed, more and more people came to do it honor, because his aunt had told everyone she met about her nephew's doing a very worthy work by order of the government. She even kept close watch so that no one would enter his room during the day. Sometimes there were a few Christians who came to adore but they tried to act as though they had just come out of curiosity.

"Oh, how wonderful! How holy! This is the first time I have ever adored before such a truly holy statue." One girl

unexpectedly betrayed her feelings and Yusa was glad there was something in his work that appealed to such a simple, unsophisticated person.

"Hagiwara-san, you will have to buy us all some sake since you are going to be rich soon."

"Your work is very fortunate; when it becomes popular it will make much money."

Not a few men said such things to him.

New Year's Day arrived and Yusa became twenty-seven years old. On New Year's morning he prayed to the rising sun. "Host of life, please let me do my work as I have always hoped to be able to do it and may it be blessed by your favor." His work progressed steadily, neither rapidly nor slowly.

"You will be able to finish it by the time of the picture-treading ceremony which we expect to hold at the end of this month, won't you?" said a government man who had come to see it.

"You see. When you try, you have a very good hand. That's why I recommended you so strongly." Magoshiro had remained away as long as he could. "It's nicely done, even though it has too strong a smell of the West, but then no one could have helped that since it is a western motif. Of course, these creases are just the same as those on your father's Archangel Michael, but it is no worse." He carefully picked up the Archangel and compared it with Yusa's creation. Yusa was now indifferent, however, to this man's way of ridiculing and belittling. It was obvious that Magoshiro, who was in-

capable of outwardly praising anything, meant that he was very much impressed.

One evening he wrote a letter to Kimika.

Dear Kimika,

Happy New Year! How are you getting along? The reason I haven't visited you for a long time is not, as you probably think, because I'm angry about your teasing. Surely I'm a dolt, but I'm a giant of a dolt so I don't care about your teasing. I've been having the busiest time I've ever had with some special work. The work I'm doing is something like what you told me to do when you gave me that medal and asked me to make a statue for you using it as a model. I appreciate your having done that because the medal is being very helpful and it gives real life to my work. Because of you I think I'll be convinced that I have created something worthwhile for the first time in my life, and at the same time I'll probably make as much money as I would need to redeem one special girl. But since I'm not sincere I'm not going to redeem you. Once I thought I would, but now I'll give you to that red-headed dog.

Tonight I feel like seeing you, but I've decided not to tempt fate. My work will be finished tomorrow and the god of work is very unpredictable and just as mischievous as you are. I fear that if I go to you he may curse me the day before I finish it and my work will be destroyed. So I'll be continent today. When I pass this milestone, how-

ever, I'll come to you even though you may hate it.

Good luck! My body is very skinny now, but I'm full of life and I still have enough power to say disagreeable things.

From an insincere man.

The next morning the work was finished. It was the twenty-fifth day after Christmas. Three government agents came and Yusa uncovered the Bronze Christ to show them.

"Oh, is this it?" The three men seemed startled and they looked at each other after they compared the statue's face with Yusa's.

"Nicely done," two of them said together.

"May we take it today?" said the third.

"No, I've made only one so far," Yusa replied. "Please wait until I make two or three copies."

"But I'd like to show this to the high commissioner. He has been looking forward to seeing it. May I just borrow it for today?"

Yusa couldn't refuse, but he cautioned, "Please take good care of it," and he gave it to them reluctantly.

The three government men went back with the religious statue. They were quite perplexed and concerned. . . .

CHAPTER 16

FOR SEVERAL days he heard no word from the high commissioner. The statue was not returned and Yusa grew perturbed. He wanted a chance to admire at close range his newly finished work, this time not as the over-critical sculptor but as a simple lover of beauty. He wanted to enjoy it as much as he wished and also to show it as soon as possible to other people, especially to Kichi and his sister. "It's too lovely a pearl for those pigs." He became angry at the high commissioner's heartlessness and almost decided to go and demand its return.

But that same night, after he went to bed very late as usual, he was tortured by insomnia which had become worse since he had started his work. He felt as though he were outdoors with a winter wind blowing, although inside his house it was really perfectly quiet except for his aunt's snoring from the next room. Suddenly someone knocked on his window. Yusa, who had just begun to doze off, opened his eyes wide in surprise and listened intently. He thought perhaps it was just a broken branch tapping against his window in the wind. But again the sound came. This time he decided it must be someone knocking. "If it is a man, who could it be?" he thought. In his brain a thousand images, good and fearful, were all intermingled but soon the latter ones became stronger and stronger.

"Maybe it is Kichi—that could only mean bad news." He stood up drawing his clothes around him and opened the window. "Who is it?" He stared at the darkness.

"Me." A short way off a girl removed her black scarf.

"Kimika!" he cried out instantly and rubbed his eyes. "Wh-what has happened?"

"Hush. Be quiet," Kimika said, looking around. "Come out here. Bad news."

"What?" He jumped out and closed the window.

"Bad news. If you waste any time you will be captured to-morrow. So hurry and come with me."

"What's the matter? What has happened?"

"They were discussing your Bronze Christ in the high commissioner's office and they decided you were a Christian."

Yusa did not understand what she meant at all. "I know you can't understand, but it was too well done. Of course, I haven't seen it but the government people were struck by the religious feeling behind your work. They say if they use it, not only will the Christians refuse to step on it but their faith will be deepened. And finally they decided you must be a Christian for no one but a Christian could make such a divine statue."

"What a farce." Yusa was stupefied. "But how did you find out?"

"From that red-headed dog."

"Red-headed dog? Ferreira?"

"Yes. You are so blind. Haven't you realized yet why I pretended to pet him?"

"Oh?"

"That's why I called you a dolt," the girl said somewhat impatiently. "Even I didn't expect it would turn out like this, but I felt it would probably be useful to catch the dog and make him tame. By abusing you I learned practically everything from him."

"Really? When?"

"This evening—just a few minutes ago. The dog has gone mad recently and has been my steady customer."

"What a crazy dog. But even though they have already made up their minds, I think it will be all right if I speak to them."

"What? How naïve you are! What could you say to them? If only your word were worth something I wouldn't worry. But do you really think you can go there and explain your complicated feelings and expect them to believe you?—not those dogs!"

"Well, then, the only way left is to flee." Yusa remained quiet for a while, thinking, and then said, "It's a little surprising but I think I'd even go to a desert island as long as it was with you. . . . Wait just a minute. I'll be right back."

"Are you going to get something? You don't have time," the girl said. "If it's money, I have some. Run. right now."

"But where?"

"Go to Amakusa Island, my homeland. Over there are thousands of little islands and it's the only place the inquisition can't reach you. Go to my house and wait for a while. I'll let you know what happens."

"Aren't you going too?"

"I can't go, much as I want to. Because I came out tonight a search has already started. They are upset and looking for me, and if I'm arrested you will be captured for sure."

"How can I go there alone? I'd die of anger and loneliness. If you are captured I'll be glad to be taken too."

"There's no time for arguing. However, I'll go with you for a little way. Here, wear my coat." The couple started to run to Urigami against the darkness and wind.

He couldn't believe it was really happening to him. All this was too fantastic to take seriously. Escaping in the moonlight with the girl he had planned on redeeming fired his young romantic imagination, but his feelings were not unmixed and he was a little frightened. When they came near the tearoom on the pass, she said, "You wait here. They are probably there already. I'll go first and see. Don't come with me." She advanced alone, peeped into the house and beckoned to him.

"How did it happen? If all this is real and not a joke, who has the right to put me in such a situation?" When he thought of this Yusa began to get angry and somewhat frantic. He was about to follow her and enter the tearoom when she suddenly screamed.

"Let go of my hand. I'll go quietly."

"If you are alone, I'll be only too glad to let you go." said the man, pushing her insultingly and rubbing his hand where she had bitten it. "But isn't there someone else? A lover, with whom you are attempting to elope perhaps?"

"Here he is." Yusa came forth, "What is the meaning of this?"

The two men smiled at each other and released the girl. "Just as we expected. Well, lover, we don't want the mare right now, but we are interested in her rider." The man who spoke was the same man whom Yusa had restrained on Christmas night. "Didn't you say you were a Christian before?"

"Yes, but only to help them. What if I were a Christian, what would it mean to you?"

"Nothing, not to me, but they say it is important to the country."

"You think he is a Christian? You need glasses. What a stupid oaf." Kimika burst out laughing. "If he were a Christian would he make a weapon that kills his own friends? What a stupid official you are. Can't you see this?"

"It's not my job to know or care whether officials are stupid or clever. Just come with me."

Yusa sat absorbed in thought in a kind of depression as he drank a cup of tea which the surprised waitress had brought him. He finally expressed his thoughts. "Very well. I'll go with you. I'll go. But if you suspect I'm a Christian won't it be all right when I step on the statue."

"But they say the sin of the one who made the statue is far graver than that of the man who does not step on it."

"What?" Kimika cried out before Yusa could. "If that is so, why bother at all with the treading picture? If you insist on being so stupid you don't have to go to all that trouble.

Why don't you just kill all the people you suspect? It would be more in keeping with your nature."

"I agree. I think you are quite logical," the man said. "Tell that to the high commissioner and I bet you will be released."

"Well, go on back to your house. Your master is awfully worried because his Golden Goose has disappeared," the other man said. "Maybe you will be able to see your lover here tomorrow night. Then you can celebrate with lots of sake. Good luck."

"There is no use trying to escape. The whole town is surrounded by a human net," the man said to Yusa. "The best thing for you to do is to come quietly."

Then the four left the tearoom. . . .

CHAPTER 17

YUSA'S EXTREME haughtiness was a great disadvantage when he appeared before the high commissioner's court and his handicap was even greater because of the desire for revenge on the part of the man whom he had seized on Christmas.

"Nevertheless, any party not treading on the picture must be punished. It is the rule, because it has the simple meaning that he is a Christian who has disobeyed the nation's law; in other words, he is a traitor. I think you are cognizant of this, are you not? And it is reported you declared to this man that you were a traitor." The high commissioner's voice droned on and on.

"But," interrupted Yusa, "I understood the reason you began to suspect me was the Bronze Christ which, I would like to point out, I made at your order. Well, I'll step on it; I'll even smash it to pieces in front of your eyes if you wish." He also repeated what Kimika had said to the other man.

"No, we recognize that the statue is very well done," the high commissioner said. "We will guard that masterpiece carefully because only something that good will detect Christians accurately. And accordingly we will always remember your distinguished service. But . . ." and here even the high commissioner hesitated before adding, "it has been a very peculiar

course you have followed. However, be that as it may, the dedication you showed in that statue is far stronger, far deeper and much more awesome than any other believer's we have seen as yet. As everyone here knows, it is with the deepest regret that we have to pass a sentence of death upon you because we believe you are an important figure—as strong as a priest." The high commissioner sighed deeply and looked around the room for approval.

"But it is too . . ." Yusa said, softening his voice again.

"No, it is enough in a way to execute you, but we must strive for perfection. Of course, our sentence is based merely on a personal opinion. And, in the coming picture-treading ceremony, because a judge is not supposed to depend on his own opinion and because we think it is important to get the actual proof, if your masterpiece does measure up to our expectation, you will lose your life because of your artistic triumph. If we are disappointed, your life will be spared." With that the judge had finished.

That same evening a rumor was spread all over Nagasaki that Yusa Hagiwara, the maker of a treading picture, had been mercifully sentenced to be beheaded in secret. . . .

CHAPTER 18

THE CEREMONY of the picture treading was solemnly begun on the twenty-eighth of January and continued for four days using Yusa's Bronze Christ. In the first three days fifteen people appeared who could not step on it. Such a thing had no precedent. On the last day, after four people had been arrested and held for further investigation, Monika arrived in a completely white dress. Her long black hair was tied in only one place and streamed down her back. At the center of the field, which had been well cleaned and sprinkled with water, there was a straw mat on which a very low table with the Bronze Christ on it had been placed. On two sides of the table sat two men who meticulously watched everyone's steps with tired eyes.

About two thousand people had already finished the examination that day and the sun was about to set. With much poise and serenity Monika slowly walked forward. She picked up the statue, held it in her hands and looked at it.

"Oh, you *have* had the faith, just as I thought. Thank you!" Monika murmured so quietly that even the officials could not hear. Suddenly she embraced the statue and covered it with kisses. Then she replaced it on the table, knelt before it and prayed. Of course, she was arrested at once.

Kimika followed next. She did the same thing and she said to the official who came to arrest her, "I'm not a believer, I swear, but I can't step on this statue. As a member of the human race I can't do that. Go ahead and arrest me, you Dogs of Hell!" And as she was led away, she continued, "At last, I'm happy. I've been waiting a long time for today."

The next evening twenty-one new crosses were erected on the execution grounds on Mt. Tateyama, and, after a prisoner was fixed upon each cross, two more men were brought out from a hidden place—Antonio Rubino and Yusa Hagiwara. When their masks were taken off two girls cried out from the crosses and one of them fell in a faint and died. Kimika had taken no food at all for seven days. The Elder's mouth had been gagged so that he would not be able to preach to the people.

"Oh, my Elder, you don't have to say anything anymore. We have won. Heaven is ours alone."

"Oh, what a glorious joy it is," Monika cried in the smoke.

When Yusa saw a man approaching with a sword, he suddenly kicked wildly at his chest and ran straight to the fence, crying out, "Help me! Help me, someone! Someone! Kichizaburo!" His bloodshot eyes searched for his friend crazily as if he expected an impossible reprieve, but his hands were tied to a long tether and he was jerked off his feet. He sat up and when he lifted his foot again to kick the man who had come to capture him, someone said from behind, "I'll help you—out of mercy," and a sword pierced his chest. He collapsed, still kicking his foot. Yusa died, a puppet of a strange fate, and with only one work, the Bronze Christ, as his offering to this

world in return for twenty-seven years of life.

Just then in another part of the execution grounds a wood-block painter was painting a caricature called "Death of Two Girls and a Western Caster." "There. Because of them, I made a masterpiece." Putting his brush back in his belt the man showed a fresh picture of cruelty to all the officials and laughed scornfully with a big mouth. "Everything is funny. Even I am funny."

But Monika was wrong when she had said, "You *have* had the faith, just as I thought."

Yusa Hagiwara was never a Christian, not even at the last. He was nothing more than a western-style caster.

DATE DUE

GAYLORD   PRINTED IN U.S.A.